Vladimir Nabokov was born in 1899 in Russia and died in 1977 in Switzerland, where his wife, Véra, still lives. An exile whose passport was his art and who spent more than fifty years as a writer, he left a legacy that includes *Glory*, *Despair*, *Laughter in the Dark*, *The Real Life of Sebastian Knight*, *Pnin*, *Pale Fire*, *Ada*, and *Speak, Memory*, as well as countless stories, poems, essays, and scholarly articles about his cherished pursuit, butterfly hunting.

Dmitri Nabokov was born in 1934 in Berlin and came to the United States as a small child. He graduated from Harvard, served in the US Army, and then began the vocal studies that led him to become an opera and concert performer – a basso – around the world. He has translated most of his father's Russian short stories and plays and many of his novels into English and has translated several works into Italian as well. The author of numerous articles and essays on Vladimir Nabokov and other subjects, he is writing a pseudonymous novel. Dmitri Nabokov also races boats and cars, climbs mountains, and skis. He lives in Montreux, Switzerland; Monza, Italy; and Palm Beach, Florida.

Also by Vladimir Nabokov
in Picador

Lectures on Literature
Lectures on Russian Literature

Vladimir Nabokov

The Enchanter
translated by Dmitri Nabokov

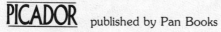 published by Pan Books

First published in Great Britain 1987 by Pan Books Ltd
Cavaye Place, London SW10 9PG
9 8 7 6 5 4 3 2 1

ISBN 0 330 29666 3

Printed in Great Britain by
Redwood Burn, Trowbridge, Wiltshire

CONTENTS

The Enchanter

AUTHOR'S NOTE ONE[1]

THE FIRST LITTLE THROB of *Lolita* went through me late in 1939 or early in 1940[2] in Paris, at a time when I was laid up with a severe attack of intercostal neuralgia. As far as I can recall, the initial shiver of inspiration was somehow prompted by a newspaper story about an ape in the Jardin des Plantes who, after months of coaxing

---

[1]Excerpt from "On a Book Entitled *Lolita*," originally published in French in *L'Affaire Lolita,* Paris, Olympia, 1957, and subsequently appended to the novel.

[2]It has been established from the manuscript of *The Enchanter* that the year was 1939.

by a scientist, produced the first drawing ever charcoaled by an animal: this sketch showed the bars of the poor creature's cage. The impulse I record had no textual connection with the ensuing train of thought, which resulted, however, in a prototype of my present novel, a short story some thirty pages long.[3] I wrote it in Russian, the language in which I had been writing novels since 1924 (the best of these are not translated into English,[4] and all are prohibited for political reasons in Russia[5]). The man was a central European, the anonymous nymphet was French, and the loci were Paris and Provence. [A brief synopsis of the plot follows, wherein Nabokov names the protagonist: he thought of him as Arthur, a name that may have appeared in some long-lost draft but is mentioned nowhere in the only known manuscript.] I read the story one blue-papered[6] wartime night to a group of friends— Mark Aldanov, two social revolutionaries,[7] and a woman doctor[8]; but I was not pleased with the thing and destroyed it sometime after moving to America in 1940.

[3]Father had not seen the story for years, and his recollection had telescoped its length somewhat.

[4]This has since been remedied.

[5]This was true until July 1986, when the Soviet literary establishment apparently realized at last that Socialist Realism and artistic reality do not necessarily coincide, and an organ of that establishment took a sharply angled turn with the announcement that "it is high time to return V. Nabokov to our readers."

[6]As an air-raid precaution.

[7]Vladimir Zenzinov and Ilya Fondaminsky.

[8]Madame Kogan-Bernstein.

Around 1949, in Ithaca, upstate New York, the throbbing, which had never quite ceased, began to plague me again. Combination joined inspiration with fresh zest and involved me in a new treatment of the theme, this time in English—the language of my first governess in St. Petersburg, circa 1903, a Miss Rachel Home. The nymphet, now with a dash of Irish blood, was really much the same lass, and the basic marrying-her-mother idea also subsisted; but otherwise the thing was new and had grown in secret the claws and wings of a novel.

VLADIMIR NABOKOV

1956

AUTHOR'S NOTE TWO[1]

As I EXPLAINED in my essay appended to *Lolita,* I had written a kind of pre-*Lolita* novella in the autumn of 1939 in Paris. I was sure I had destroyed it long ago but today, as Véra and I were collecting some additional material to give to the Library of Congress, a single copy of the story turned up. My first movement was to deposit it (and a

[1]Excerpt from a letter of 6 February 1959, in which Nabokov proposed *The Enchanter* to Walter Minton, then president of G. P. Putnam's Sons. Minton's reply expressed keen interest, but apparently the manuscript was never sent. Father was engrossed at the time in *Eugene Onegin, Ada,* the *Lolita* screenplay, and checking my translation of *Invitation to a Beheading.* He probably decided there was no room in his schedule for an additional project.

batch of index cards with unused *Lolita* material) at the L. of C., but then something else occurred to me.

The thing is a story of fifty-five typewritten pages in Russian, entitled *Volshebnik* ("The Enchanter"). Now that my creative connection with *Lolita* is broken, I have re-read *Volshebnik* with considerably more pleasure than I experienced when recalling it as a dead scrap during my work on *Lolita*. It is a beautiful piece of Russian prose, precise and lucid, and with a little care could be done into English by the Nabokovs.

VLADIMIR NABOKOV

1959

TRANSLATOR'S NOTE

IN THE INTEREST of clarifying certain concentrated images (some of which originally stumped me too), and of providing the curious reader with a few informative sidelights, I have prepared a short commentary. In the interest of letting the reader get on with the story, I have placed my comments at the end and have, with one exception, avoided the distraction of footnotes in the text itself.

The Enchanter

"How can I come to terms with myself?" he thought, when he did any thinking at all. "This cannot be lechery. Coarse carnality is omnivorous; the subtle kind presupposes eventual satiation. So what if I did have five or six normal affairs—how can one compare their insipid randomness with my unique flame? What is the answer? It certainly isn't like the arithmetic of Oriental debauchery, where the tenderness of the prey is inversely proportional to its age. Oh, no, to me it's not a degree of a generic whole, but something totally divorced from the generic, something that is not *more* valuable but *in*valuable. What is it then? Sickness, criminality? And is it compatible with conscience and shame, with squeamishness and fear, with self-control and sensitivity? For I cannot even consider the thought of causing pain or provoking unforgettable revulsion. Nonsense—I'm no ravisher. The limitations I have established for my yearning, the masks I invent for it when, in real life, I conjure up an absolutely invisible method of sating my passion, have a providential sophistry. I am a pickpocket, not a burglar. Although, perhaps, on a circular island, with my little female Friday . . . (it would not be a question of mere safety, but a license to grow savage— or is the circle a vicious one, with a palm tree at its center?).

"Knowing, rationally, that the Euphrates apricot[1] is harmful only in canned form; that sin is inseparable from civic custom; that all hygienes have their hyenas; knowing, moreover, that this selfsame rationality is not averse to vulgarizing that to which it is otherwise denied access . . . I now discard all that and ascend to a higher plane.

"What if the way to true bliss is indeed through a still delicate membrane, before it has had time to harden, become overgrown, lose the fragrance and the shimmer through which one penetrates to the throbbing star of that bliss? Even within these limitations I proceed with

[1]Thought by some to have been the true identity of the Biblical apple— D.N.

a refined selectivity; I'm not attracted to every schoolgirl that comes along, far from it—how many one sees, on a gray morning street, that are husky, or skinny, or have a necklace of pimples or wear spectacles—*those* kinds interest me as little, in the amorous sense, as a lumpy female acquaintance might interest someone else. In any case, independently of any special sensations, I feel at home with children in general, in all simplicity; I know that I would be a most loving father in the common sense of the word, and to this day cannot decide whether this is a natural complement or a demonic contradiction.

"Here I invoke the law of degrees that I repudiated where I found it insulting: often I have tried to catch myself in the transition from one kind of tenderness to the other, from the simple to the special, and would very much like to know whether they are mutually exclusive, whether they must, after all, be assigned to different genera, or whether one is a rare flowering of the other on the Walpurgis Night of my murky soul; for, if they are two separate entities, then there must be two separate kinds of beauty, and the aesthetic sense, invited to dinner, sits down with a crash between two chairs (the fate of any dualism). On the other hand, the return journey, from the special to the simple, I find somewhat more comprehensible: the former is subtracted, as it were, at the moment it is quenched, and that would seem to indicate that the sum of sensations is indeed homogeneous, if in fact the rules of arithmetic are applicable here. It is a strange, strange thing—and strangest of all, perhaps, is that, under the pretext of discussing something remarkable, I am merely seeking justification for my guilt."

Thus, more or less, fidgeted his thoughts. He was fortunate enough to have a refined, precise, and rather lucrative profession, one that refreshed his mind, sated his sense of touch, nourished his eyesight with a vivid point on black velvet. There were numbers here, and colors, and entire crystal systems. On occasion his imagination would remain chained for months, and the chain would give only an occasional clink. Besides, having, by the age of forty, tormented himself sufficiently with his fruitless self-immolation, he had learned to regulate his longing and had hypocritically resigned himself to the notion that only a most fortunate combination of circumstances, a hand most inadvertently dealt him by fate, could result in a momentary semblance of the impossible.

His memory treasured those few moments with melancholy gratitude (they had, after all, been bestowed) and melancholy irony (he had, after all, outsmarted life). Thus, back in his student days at the polytechnic, while helping a classmate's younger sister—a sleepy, wan girl with a velvety gaze and a pair of black pigtails—to cram geometry, he had never once brushed against her, but the very nearness of her woolen dress was enough to start making the lines on the paper quiver and dissolve, to cause everything to shift into a different dimension at a tense, clandestine jog—and afterward, once again, there was the hard chair, the lamp, the scribbling schoolgirl. His other lucky moments had been of the same laconic genre: a fidget with a lock of hair over one eye in a leather-upholstered office where he was waiting to see her father (the pounding in his chest—"Say, are you ticklish?"); or that other one, with shoulders the color of gingerbread, showing him, in a crossed-out corner of a sunlit courtyard, some black salad devouring a green rabbit. These had been pitiful, hurried moments, separated by years of roaming and searching, yet he would have paid anything for any one of them (intermediaries, however, were asked to abstain).

Recalling those extreme rarities, those little mistresses of his, who had never even noticed the incubus, he also marveled at how he had remained mysteriously ignorant of their subsequent fate; and yet, how many times, on a shabby lawn, on a vulgar city bus, or on some seaside sand useful only as food for an hourglass, he had been betrayed by a grim, hasty choice, his entreaties had been ignored by chance, and the delight of his eyes interrupted by a heedless turn of events.

Thin, dry-lipped, with a slightly balding head and ever watchful eyes, he now seated himself on a bench in a city park. July abolished the clouds, and a minute later he put on the hat he had been holding in his white, slender-fingered hands. The spider pauses, the heartbeat halts.

On his left sat an elderly brunette with a ruddy fore-head, dressed in mourning; on his right a woman with limp, dull-blond hair was knitting industriously. His gaze mechanically followed the flitting of children in the col-ored haze, and he was thinking about other things—his current work, the attractive shape of his new footwear—when he happened to notice, near his heel, a large nickel coin, partially defaced by the pebbles. He picked it up. The mustachioed female on his left did not respond to his natural question; the colorless one on his right said:

"Tuck it away. It means good luck on odd-numbered days."

"Why only on odd-numbered days?"

"That's what they say where I come from, in———"

She named a town where he had once admired the ornate architecture of a diminutive black church.

"...Oh, we live on the other side of the river. The hillside is full of vegetable gardens, it's lovely, there isn't any dust or noise...."

A talkative one, he thought—looks like I'll have to move.

And at this point the curtain rises.

A violet-clad girl of twelve (he never erred), was tread-ing rapidly and firmly on skates that did not roll but

crunched on the gravel as she raised and lowered them
with little Japanese steps and approached his bench through
the variable luck of the sunlight. Subsequently (for as long
as the sequel lasted), it seemed to him that right away, at
that very moment, he had appreciated all of her from tip
to toe: the liveliness of her russet curls (recently trimmed);
the radiance of her large, slightly vacuous eyes, somehow
suggesting translucent gooseberries; her merry, warm
complexion; her pink mouth, slightly open so that two
large front teeth barely rested on the protuberance of
the lower lip; the summery tint of her bare arms with the
sleek little foxlike hairs running along the forearms; the
indistinct tenderness of her still narrow but already not
quite flat chest; the way the folds of her skirt moved;
their succinctness and soft concavities; the slenderness and
glow of her uncaring legs; the coarse straps of the skates.

She stopped in front of his garrulous neighbor, who
turned away to rummage in something lying to her right,
then produced a slice of bread with a piece of chocolate
on it and handed it to the girl. The latter, chewing rapidly,
used her free hand to undo the straps and with them the
entire weighty mass of the steel soles and solid wheels.
Then, returning to earth among the rest of us, she stood
up with an instantaneous sensation of heavenly barefootedness, not immediately recognizable as the feel of skate-
less shoes, and went off, now hesitantly, now with easy
strides, until finally (probably because she had done with

the bread) she took off at full tilt, swinging her liberated arms, flashing in and out of sight, mingling with a kindred play of light beneath the violet-and-green trees.

"Your daughter," he remarked senselessly, "is a big girl already."

"Oh, no—we're not related," said the knitter. "I don't have any of my own, and don't regret it."

The old woman in mourning broke into sobs and left. The knitter looked after her and continued working quickly, now and then, with a lightning motion, adjusting the trailing tail of her woolen fetus. Was it worth continuing the conversation?

The heel plates of the skates glistened by the foot of the bench, and the tan straps stared him in the face. That stare was the stare of life. His despair was now compounded. Superimposed on all his still-vivid past despairs, there was now a new and special monster. . . . No, he must not stay. He tipped his hat ("So long," replied the knitter in a friendly tone) and walked away across the square. Despite his sense of self-preservation a secret wind kept blowing him to one side, and his course, originally conceived as a straight traverse, deviated to the right, toward the trees. Even though he knew from experience that one more look would simply exacerbate his hopeless longing, he completed his turn into the iridescent shade, his eyes furtively seeking the violet speck among the other colors.

On the asphalt lane there was a deafening clatter of

roller skates. A private game of hopscotch was in progress at its curb. And there, waiting her turn, with one foot extended to the side, her blazing arms crossed on her chest, her misty head inclined, emanating a fierce, chestnut heat, losing, losing the layer of violet that disintegrated into ashes under his terrible, unnoticed gaze . . . Never before, though, had the subordinate clause of his fearsome life been complemented by the principal one, and he walked past with clenched teeth, stifling his exclamations and his moans, then gave a passing smile to a toddler who had run between his scissorlike legs.

"Absentminded smile," he thought pathetically. "Then again, only *humans* are capable of absentmindedness."

AT DAYBREAK HE DROWSILY laid down his book like a dead fish folding its fin, and suddenly began berating himself: why, he demanded, did you succumb to the doldrums of despair, why didn't you try to get a proper conversation going, and then make friends with that knitter, chocolate-woman, governess or whatever; and he pictured a jovial gentleman (whose internal organs only, for the moment, resembled his own) who could thus gain the opportunity—thanks to that very joviality—to collect you-naughty-little-girl-you onto his lap. He knew that he was not very sociable, but also that he was resourceful, persistent, and capable of ingratiating himself; more than once, in other areas of his life, he had had to improvise a tone or apply himself tenaciously, undismayed that his immediate target was at best only indirectly related to his more remote goal. But when the goal blinds you, suffocates you, parches your throat, when healthy shame and sickly cowardice scrutinize your every step . . .

She was clattering across the asphalt amid the others, leaning well forward and rhythmically swinging her relaxed arms, hurtling past with confident speed. She turned deftly, and her thigh was bared by the flip of her skirt. Then her dress clung so closely in back that it outlined a small cleft as, with a barely perceptible undulation of her calves, she rolled slowly backward. Was it concupiscence, this torment he experienced as he consumed her with his eyes, marveling at her flushed face, at the compactness and perfection of her every movement (particularly when, having barely frozen motionless, she dashed off again, pumping swiftly with her prominent knees)? Or else was it the anguish that always accompanied his hopeless yearning to extract something from beauty, to hold it still for an instant, to do something with it—no matter what, provided there were some kind of contact, that somehow, no matter how, could quench that yearning? Why puzzle over it? She'd gather speed again and vanish—and tomorrow a different one would flash by, and thus, in a succession of disappearances, his life would pass.

Or would it? He saw the same woman knitting on the same bench and, sensing that, instead of a gentlemanly smile, he had leered and flashed a tusk from beneath a bluish lip, sat down. His uneasiness and the trembling of his hands did not last long. A conversation developed, which in itself gave him a strange satisfaction; the weight on his chest dissolved, and he began to feel almost merry. She appeared, clamping along on her skates, as she had the previous day. Her light-gray eyes dwelled on him for an instant, even though it was not he but the knitter who was speaking, and, having accepted him, she turned insouciantly away. Then she was sitting beside him, holding onto the edge of the seat with rosy, sharp-knuckled hands, on which shifted now a vein, now a deep dimple near the wrist while her hunched shoulders remained motionless, and her dilating pupils followed someone's ball rolling across the gravel. As the day before, his neighbor, reaching across him, handed a sandwich to the girl, who began tapping her somewhat scarred knees together lightly as she ate.

"... her health, of course; but, most of all, a first-rate school," a distant voice was saying when he suddenly noticed that the auburn-curled head on his left had silently bent low over his hand.

"You lost the hands of your watch," said the girl.

"No," he answered, clearing his throat, "that's the way it's supposed to be. It's a rarity."

Reaching across with her left hand (the right one was holding the sandwich) she caught hold of his wrist and examined the blank, centerless dial beneath which the hands were inserted, revealing only their very tips, like two black droplets, amid the silvery digits. A shriveled leaf trembled in her hair, very near her neck above the delicate projection of a vertebra—and during his next spell of insomnia he kept yanking off the ghost of that leaf, grasping and yanking, with two fingers, with three, then with all five.

The day after, and the days that followed, he sat in the same place, doing an amateurish but quite tolerable imitation of an eccentric loner: the usual hour, the usual place. The girl's arrival, her breathing, her legs, her hair, everything she did, whether it was scratching a shin and leaving white marks on it, or throwing a small black ball high in the air, or brushing against him with a bare elbow as she seated herself on the bench—all of it (while he appeared engrossed in pleasant conversation) evoked an intolerable sensation of sanguine, dermal, multivascular communion with her, as if the monstrous bisector pumping all the juices from the depths of his being extended into her like a pulsating dotted line, as if this girl were growing out of him, as if, with every carefree movement, she tugged and shook her vital roots implanted in the bowels of his being, so that, when she abruptly changed position or rushed off, he felt a yank, a barbarous pluck, a momentary loss of equilibrium: suddenly you are traveling through the dust on your back, banging the back of your head, on your way to being strung up by your insides. And all the while he calmly sat listening, smiling, nodding his head, pulling at a pant leg to free his knee, scrabbling lightly in the gravel with his walking stick, and saying, "Is that so?" or "Yes, it happens sometimes, you know . . . ," but comprehending his neighbor's words only when the girl was nowhere nearby. He learned from this circumstantiating chatterbox that between her and the girl's mother, a forty-two-year-old widow, there existed a five-year friendship (her own husband's honor had been saved by the widow's late spouse); that last spring this widow had, after a long illness, undergone a serious operation of the intestine; that, having long since lost all her family, she had promptly and tenaciously clutched at the kind couple's suggestion that the girl move in with them in their provincial town; and that now she had been brought for a visit with her mother, as the garrulous lady's husband had a bit of bothersome business to attend to in the capital, but that soon it would be time to head home—the sooner the better, for the girl's presence only irritated the widow, who was exceptionally decent but had grown somewhat self-indulgent.

"Say, didn't you mention that she was selling off some sort of furniture?"

This question (with its continuation) he had prepared during the night and tried out sotto voce on the ticking silence; having convinced himself that it sounded natural, he repeated it the next day to his newfound acquaintance. She replied affirmatively and explained in no uncertain terms that it wouldn't be a bad idea if the widow made a little money—her medical care was costing and would continue to cost a lot, her resources were very limited, she insisted on paying for her daughter's upkeep but did so rather sporadically—and we're not rich either—in a word, the debt of honor, apparently, was considered already extinguished.

"Actually," he continued without missing a beat, "I could use certain pieces of furniture myself. Do you suppose it might be convenient as well as proper if I . . ." He had forgotten the rest of his sentence, but improvised most adroitly, as he was beginning to feel at home with the artificial style of the still not fully comprehensible, many-ringed dream with which he was already so indistinctly but so firmly entwined that, for instance, he no longer knew what this thing was, and whose: part of his own leg or part of an octopus.

She was obviously delighted, and offered to take him there that very moment if he wished—the widow's apartment, where she and her husband were also staying, was not far, right on the other side of the electric-railway bridge.

They set off. The girl walked in front, energetically swinging a canvas bag on a string, and already everything about her was, to his eyes, terrifyingly and insatiably familiar—the curve of her narrow back, the resilience of the two round little muscles farther down, the exact way the checks of her dress (the other, brown, one) tightened when she raised an arm, the delicate ankles, the rather high heels. She might be a little introverted, livelier of movement than of conversation, neither bashful nor forward, with a soul that seemed submerged, but in a radiant moistness. Opalescent on the surface but translucent in her depths, she must be fond of sweets, and puppies, and the innocent trickery of newsreels. Such warm-skinned, russet-sheened, open-lipped girls got their periods early, and it was little more to them than a game, like cleaning up a dollhouse kitchen. . . . And hers was not a very happy childhood, that of a half-orphan: this stern woman's kindness was not like milk chocolate, but like the bitter kind— a home without caresses, strict order, symptoms of fatigue, a favor for a friend grown burdensome. . . . And for all this, for the glow of her cheeks, the twelve pairs of narrow ribs, the down along her back, her wisp of a soul, that slightly husky voice, the roller skates and the grayish day, the unknown thought that had just run through her head as she glanced at an unknown thing from the bridge . . . For all this he would have given a sack of rubies, a bucket of blood, anything he was asked. . . .

Outside the building they ran into an unshaven man with a briefcase, as unabashed and as gray as his wife, so the four of them made a noisy entrance together. He expected to find a sick, emaciated woman in an armchair, but instead was met by a tall, pale, broad-hipped lady, with a hairless wart near a nostril of her bulbous nose: one of those faces you describe without being able to say anything about the lips or the eyes because any mention of them even this—would be an involuntary contradiction of their utter inconspicuousness.

Upon learning that he was a potential buyer she immediately ushered him into the dining room, explaining, as she proceeded slowly and with a slight list, that she had no need for a four-room apartment, that she was moving that winter into a two-room one, and that she would be glad to get rid of that extension table, the extra chairs, that couch over in the parlor (when it had done its duty as a sleeping accommodation for her friends), a large étagère, and a small chest. He said he would like to see the last of these items, which turned out to be in the room occupied by the girl, whom they found lolling on the bed and gazing at the ceiling, with her knees, drawn up and encircled by outstretched arms, rocking in unison.

"Off the bed! What's the meaning of this?" Hurriedly

concealing the soft skin of her underside and the tiny wedge of her taut panties, she rolled off (oh, the liberties I would allow her! he thought).

He said he would buy the chest—it was a laughably cheap price for access to the house—and possibly something else as well, but he had to decide just what. If it was all right with her, he would drop by for another look in a couple of days and then have everything picked up at the same time—here, by the way, was his card.

As she saw him to the door she unsmilingly (evidently she smiled seldom) but quite cordially mentioned that her friend and her daughter had already told her about him and that her friend's husband was even a little jealous.

"Sure, sure," said the latter, following them into the vestibule. "I'd gladly unload my better half on anybody who'd take her."

"Watch your step," said his wife, appearing from the same room as he. "Someday you might be sorry!"

"Well, you're welcome anytime," said the widow. "I'm always home, and you might be interested in the lamp or the pipe collection—they are all fine things, and it makes me a little sad to part with them, but that's life."

"What next?" he wondered on the way home. Up to that point he had played it by ear, practically without forethought, following blind intuition, like a chess player penetrating and applying pressure wherever there is a hint of shakiness or constriction in his opponent's position. But what now? Day after tomorrow they are taking my darling away—that rules out any direct benefit from my acquaintance with her mother. . . . She'll be back, though, and may even stay here for good, and by that time I'll be a welcome guest. . . . But if the woman has less than a year to live (according to the hints I was given), then everything goes down the drain. . . . I must say she doesn't look too decrepit to me, but if she does take to her bed and die, then the setting and the circumstances for a potentially jovial relationship will crumble, then it will all be over—how would I find her, under what pretext? . . . Nevertheless, he felt instinctively that this was the way to proceed: don't think too much, keep the pressure on the weak corner of the board.

Therefore, next day he set out for the park with an attractive box of marrons glacés and sugar violets as a going-away present for the girl. Reason told him that it was a silly cliché, that this was a particularly dangerous moment to single her out for overt attention, even from an uninhibited eccentric, especially since so far he had— quite rightly—paid hardly any attention to her (he was a past master at dissimulating lightning bolts)—not like one of your putrid oldsters who always carry some candy to lure the lasses—and still he minced along with his present, in response to a secret impulse that was more accurate than reason.

He spent a whole hour on the bench, but they did not come. Must have left a day early. And, although one more encounter with her could in no way have alleviated the very special burden that had accumulated during the past week, he experienced the burning chagrin of a betrayed lover.

Continuing to ignore the voice of reason that told him he was again doing the wrong thing, he rushed over to the widow's and bought the lamp. Noticing his odd shortness of breath, she invited him to sit down and offered him a cigarette. In his search for a lighter he came upon the oblong box and said, like a character in a book:

"It may seem odd to you, since we've known each other for such a short time, but still allow me to present you with this trifle—a little candy, not bad candy, I think— if you accept, it will give me great pleasure."

She smiled for the first time—apparently she was more flattered than surprised—and explained that all the sweets of life were forbidden to her, and that she would give it to her daughter.

"Oh—I thought they had already—"

"No, tomorrow morning," the widow resumed, fingering the gold ribbon not without regret. "Today, my friend, who spoils her dreadfully, took her to an exhibition of handicrafts." She sighed, and gingerly, as if it were something fragile, set the gift on a nearby side table, while her exceedingly charming guest inquired what she was and was not allowed, and listened to the epic of her malady, referring to the variants and interpreting with great acuity the most recent distortions of the text.

BY THE THIRD VISIT (he had dropped by to inform her that the mover could come no earlier than Friday) he had tea with her and, in his turn, told her about himself and about his limpid, elegant profession. They turned out to have a common acquaintance, the brother of an attorney who had died the same year as her husband. Objectively and without insincere regrets she discussed the husband, about whom he already knew certain things: he had been a bon vivant and an expert on notarial matters; he had gotten on well with his wife, but had tried to spend as little time as possible at home.

On Thursday he bought the couch and the two chairs, and on Saturday he called for her as agreed to take her for a quiet stroll in the park. However, she was feeling rotten, was in bed with a hot-water bottle, and spoke to him in a singsong through the door. He asked the gloomy crone who periodically appeared to cook and nurse to let him know at such-and-such a number how the patient had spent the night.

In this fashion a few more busy weeks elapsed, weeks of murmuring, exploration, persuasion, intensive remolding of another's pliable solitude. Now he was moving toward a definite goal, for, even back when he had proffered the candy, he had suddenly recognized the outlying destination silently indicated to him by what looked like a strange, nailless finger (scrawled on a fence), and the true hiding-place of genuine, blinding opportunity. The path was unenticing but neither was it difficult, and the sight of a weekly letter to Mother, in a still unsteady, coltishly sprawling hand, left lying about with inexplicable heedlessness, sufficed to put an end to any sort of doubt.

He had learned from other sources that the mother had checked on him, with results that could only have pleased her, not the least of which was a well-kept bank account. From the way she showed him, with devoutly lowered voice, old, rigid snapshots depicting, in various more or less flattering poses, a young girl in high shoes with a round, pleasant face, a nice full bosom, and hair combed back from her forehead (there were also the wedding photos, which invariably included the bridegroom, who had a happily surprised expression and an oddly familiar slant to his eyes), he gathered that she was surreptitiously addressing the faded mirror of the past in search of something that might even now entitle her to masculine attention, and must have decided that the keen eye of an appraiser of facets and reflections could still discern the traces of her past comeliness (which, incidentally, she exaggerated), traces that would become even more apparent after this retrospective bride show.

To the cup of tea she poured him she imparted a dainty touch of intimacy; into the highly detailed accounts of her diverse indispositions she managed to infuse so much romanticism that he could barely resist asking some coarse question; and at times she would pause, seemingly lost in thought, and then catch up, with a belated query, to his cautiously tiptoeing words.

He felt both sorry and repelled but, realizing that the material, apart from its one specific function, had no potential whatever, he kept doggedly at his chore, which in itself demanded such concentration that the physical aspect of this woman dissolved and vanished (if he had run into her on the street in a different part of town he would not have recognized her) and its place was haphazardly filled by the formal features of the abstract bride in the snapshots, grown so familiar that they had lost all meaning (thus, after all, her pathetic calculations had been successful).

The task proceeded swimmingly and when, one rainy, late-fall evening, she heard out—impassively, without a single bit of feminine advice—his vague complaints about the yearnings of a bachelor who looks with envy at the tailcoat and misty aura of another's wedding and thinks involuntarily of the lonely grave at the end of his lonely road, he concluded the time had come to call the packers. Meanwhile, though, he sighed and changed the subject, and, a day later, how she was amazed when their silent tea-drinking (he had gone to the window a couple of times, as if meditating about something) was interrupted by the furniture mover's powerful ring. Home came two chairs, the couch, the lamp, and the chest: thus, when solving a mathematical problem, one first sets aside a certain number so as to work more freely, and then returns it to the womb of the solution.

"You don't understand. All it means is that a married couple's belongings are owned jointly. In other words, I offer you both the contents of the cuff and the live ace of hearts."

Meanwhile, two workmen who had brought in the furniture were bustling nearby, and she chastely retreated to the next room.

"You know something?" she said. "Go home and have a good sleep."

He tried, with a chuckle, to take her hand in his, but she drew it behind her back, repeating resolutely that this was all a lot of nonsense.

"All right," he replied, producing a handful of change and preparing the tip in his palm. "All right, I'll leave, but, if you decide to accept, kindly let me know, otherwise don't bother—I'll rid you of my presence forever."

"Wait a bit. Let them leave first. You pick strange times for this kind of talk."

"Now let's sit down and discuss things rationally," she said a moment later, having descended heavily and meekly onto the newly returned sofa (while he sat next to her in profile with one leg tucked under him, holding onto the lace of the protruding shoe). "First of all, my friend, as you know, I am a sick, a seriously sick, woman. For a couple of years now my life as been one of constant medical care. The operation I had on April twenty-fifth was in all likelihood the next-to-last one—in other words, next time they'll take me from the hospital to the cemetery. No, no, don't pooh-pooh what I'm saying. Let's even assume I last a few more years—what change can there be? I'm doomed until my dying day to suffer all the torments of my infernal diet, and my attention is totally focused on my stomach and my nerves. My character is hopelessly ruined. There was a time when I never stopped laughing. . . . Yet I have always been demanding of others, and now I'm demanding of everything—of material objects, of my neighbors' dog, of every minute of my existence that does not serve me as I want. You know that I was married for seven years. I have no recollection of any special happiness. I am a bad mother, but have reconciled myself to that, and know that my death would only be accelerated by having a boisterous girl around, and at the same time I feel a stupid, painful envy for her muscular little legs, her rosy complexion, her healthy digestion. I'm poor: one half of my pension goes for my illness, the other for my debts. Even if one were to suppose you had the kind of character and sensibilities ... oh, in a word, the various traits that might make you a suitable husband for me—see, I stress the word 'me'—what kind of existence would you have with such a wife? I may feel young spiritually, and I may not yet be a total monstrosity to look at, but won't you get bored constantly fussing with such a fastidious person, never, never contradicting her, respecting her habits and eccentricities, her fasting and the other rules she lives by? And all for what—in order to remain, perhaps in six months or so, a widower with someone else's child on your hands!"

"Which leads me to conclude," said he, "that my proposal has been accepted." And he shook out into his hand, from a chamois pouch, a splendid uncut stone that seemed illuminated from within by a rosy flame gleaming through a winy-bluish cast.

THE GIRL ARRIVED two days before the wedding, cheeks aglow and wearing an unbuttoned blue coat with the ends of its belt dangling behind, woolen stockings almost up to her knees, and a beret on her damp curls.

Yes, yes, it was worth it, he repeated mentally as he held her cold red hand and smilingly grimaced at the yelps of her inevitable companion: "I'm the one who found you a fiancé, I brought you your fiancé, I'm responsible for your fiancé!" (and she tried, in the style of an artilleryman swinging his gun, to give the unwieldy bride a whirl).

It was worth it, yes—no matter how long he would have to drag this cumbersome behemoth through the quagmire of marriage; it was worth it even if she outlived everybody; it was worth it for the sake of making his presence natural and of his license as future stepfather.

However, he did not yet know how to take advantage of that license, partly from lack of practice, partly in anticipation of incredibly greater liberty, but mainly because he could never manage to be alone with the girl. It was true that, with her mother's permission, he took her to a nearby café, and sat, with his hands propped on his walking stick, watching as she leaned forward and ate her way into the apricot edge of some latticed pastry, thrusting out her lower lip to catch the sticky flakes. He tried to make her laugh, and chat with her as he would have with an ordinary child, but his progress was continually hampered by an obstructing thought: had the room been emptier and more cosy-cornered, he would have fondled her a little, without any special pretext and with no fear of strangers' glances (more perceptive than her trustful innocence). As he walked her home, and as he lagged behind her on the stairs, he was tormented not only by a sense of missed opportunity but also by the thought that, until he had done certain specific things at least once, he could not count on the promises fate transmitted through her innocent speech, the subtle nuances of her childish common sense and her silences (when her teeth, from beneath the listening lip, pressed gently down on the pensive one), the gradual emergence of dimples on hearing old jokes that struck her as being new, and his intuitive perception of the undulations in her subterranean streams (without which she could not have had those eyes). So what if, in the future, his freedom of action, his freedom to do and repeat special things, would render everything limpid and harmonious? Meanwhile, now, today, a misprint of desire distorted the meaning of love. That dark spot represented a kind of obstacle that must be crushed, erased, as soon as possible—no matter with what forgery of bliss—so that the child might at last be aware of the joke and he might be rewarded by their having a good laugh together, by being able to take disinterested care of her, to meld the wave of fatherhood with the wave of sexual love.

Yes—the forgery, the furtiveness, the fear of the least suspicion, complaint, or innocent report ("You know, Mother, whenever nobody's around he always starts caressing"), the necessity of being on his guard so as not to fall prey to a chance hunter in these heavily populated valleys—that was what now tormented him, and what would no longer exist in the freedom of his own preserve. But when? when? he thought in despair, as he paced his quiet, familiar rooms.

The following morning he accompanied his monstrous bride to some office. Thence she was going to the doctor, evidently in order to ask certain ticklish questions, since she instructed her bridegroom to go to her apartment and expect her for dinner in an hour. His nocturnal despair was forgotten. He knew that her friend (whose husband had not come at all) was also out doing errands—and the foretaste of finding the girl alone melted like cocaine in his loins. But when he rushed into the apartment he found her chatting with the charwoman amid a compass rose of drafts. He picked up a newspaper (dated the 32nd) and, unable to distinguish the lines, sat for a long while in the already done parlor, listening to the lively conversation during pauses in the vacuum's howl in the adjoining room, glancing at the enamel of his watch as he mentally murdered the char and shipped the corpse off to Borneo. Then he heard a third voice and remembered that the old crone was in the kitchen too (he thought he heard the girl being sent to the grocer's). Then the vacuum finished its wheezing and was turned off, a window slammed shut, and the street noise ceased. He waited out another minute, then got up and, humming sotto voce, with darting eyes, began exploring the now silent apartment.

No, she had not been sent anywhere. She was standing at the window of her room looking out into the street with her palms pressed against the glass.

She looked around and quickly said, with a toss of her hair and already resuming her observation, "Look—an accident!"

He moved closer and closer, sensing with his nape that the door had shut by itself, closer to the lithe concavity of her spine, to the gathers at her waist, to the lozenge-shaped checks of the cloth whose texture he could already palpate from seven feet away, to the firm, light-blue veins above the edge of her knee-high stockings, to the whiteness of her neck sheeny from the sidewise light next to her brown curls, which received another vigorous toss (seven-eighths habit, one little eighth flirtatiousness). "Ah, an accident . . . a taxi dent . . . ," he mumbled, pretending to peer through the empty window over the crown of her head but seeing only the tiny flecks of dandruff in its silky vertex.

"It's the red one's fault!" she exclaimed with conviction.

"Ah, the red one . . . We'll get the red one," he continued incoherently and, standing in back of her, feeling faint, abolishing the final inch of the melting distance, took hold of her hands from behind and began senselessly spreading and tugging them, while she did no more than gently rotate the slender wristbone of her right hand, mechanically trying to point her finger at the guilty party. "Wait," he said hoarsely, "press your elbows against your sides and let's see if I can, if I can lift you." Just then a bang came from the vestibule followed by the ominous rustling of a raincoat, and he moved away from her with an awkward abruptness, thrusting his hands in his pockets, clearing his throat with a growl, starting to say in a loud voice, ". . . at last! We're famished here. . . ." And, as they were sitting down to table, there was still an aching, frustrated, gnawing weakness in his calves.

After dinner some ladies came for coffee, and, toward evening, when the wave of guests had receded and her faithful friend had discreetly left for the cinema, the exhausted hostess stretched out on the couch.

"Go on home, my dear," she said without raising her eyelids. "You must have things to take care of, you probably don't have anything packed, and I'd like to go to bed, or else I won't be up to doing anything tomorrow."

With a short mooing sound to simulate tenderness he pecked her on the forehead, which was cold as cottage cheese, then said, "By the way, I keep thinking how sorry I feel for the girl. I suggest we keep her here after all. Why should the poor thing have to continue staying with strangers? It's downright ludicrous now that there is a family once again. Think it over carefully, dearest."

"And I'm still sending her off tomorrow," she drawled in a feeble voice, without opening her eyes.

"Please, try to understand," he continued more softly, for the girl, who had been dining in the kitchen, had apparently finished and her faint glow was present somewhere nearby. "Try to understand what I'm saying. Even if we pay them for everything, and even overpay them, do you think that will make her feel any more at home there? I doubt it. There's a fine school there, you'll tell

me," (she was silent) "but we'll find an even better one
here, apart from the fact that I am and always have been
in favor of private instruction at home. But the main
thing is . . . you see, people might get the impression—
and you already heard one little hint of that kind just
today—that, in spite of the changed situation, i.e., now
that you have support of all kinds from me and we can
get a larger apartment, arrange complete privacy for our-
selves, and so forth, the mother and stepfather still tend
to neglect the kid."

She said nothing.

"Of course you can do as you please," he said nervously,
frightened by her silence (he had gone too far!).

"I've already told you," she drawled with that same
ridiculous, martyrlike softness, "that what is paramount
to me is my peace and quiet. If it is disrupted I shall
die. . . . Listen: there she goes scraping her foot on the
floor or banging something—it wasn't very loud, was
it?—yet it's already enough to give me a nervous spasm
and make me see spots before my eyes. And a child cannot
live without banging around; even if there are twenty-
five rooms all twenty-five will be noisy. Therefore you'll
have to choose between me and her."

"No, no—don't even say such things!" he cried with
a panicky catch in his throat. "There isn't even any question of choosing. . . . Heaven forbid! It was just a theoretical consideration. You're right. All the more so, because

I, too, value peace and quiet. Yes! I'm in favor of the status quo, and let the gossips keep jabbering. You're right, dearest. Of course, I don't rule out that perhaps later on, next spring . . . if you're quite well again . . ."

"I'll never be quite well," she answered softly, raising herself and, with a creak, rolling heavily onto her side. Then she propped up her cheek with her fist and, with a shake of her head and an oblique glance, repeated the same sentence.

The next day, following the civil ceremony and a moderately festive dinner, the girl left after having twice, in front of everyone, touched his shaven cheek with her cool, unhurried lips: once over the champagne glass to congratulate him, and then at the door, as she was saying good-bye. After which he brought over his suitcases and spent a long time arranging his things in her former room where, in a bottom drawer, he found a little rag of hers that told him far more than those two incomplete kisses.

Judging by the tone that the person (he found the appellation "wife" inapplicable to her) used to emphasize how it was generally more convenient to sleep in separate rooms (he did not argue) and how she herself, incidentally, was accustomed to sleeping alone (he let it go by), he could not avoid the conclusion that that very night he was expected to be instrumental in the first infraction of that habit. As the murk gradually thickened outside the window, and he felt increasingly foolish sitting next to

her couch in the parlor, wordlessly compressing or applying to his tense jowl her ominously obedient hand,
with bluish freckles on its glossy back, he perceived ever
more clearly that the moment of reckoning had arrived,
that now no escape remained from what he had of course
long foreseen, but without giving it much thought (when
the moment comes I'll manage somehow); now that moment was knocking at the door and it was perfectly clear
that he (little Gulliver) would be physically unable to
tackle those broad bones, those multiple caverns, the bulky
velvet, the formless anklebones, the repulsively listing con-
formation of her ponderous pelvis, not to mention the
rancid emanations of her wilted skin and the as yet un-
disclosed miracles of surgery ... here his imagination was
left hanging on barbed wire.

Already at dinner, first refusing a second glass with an
apparent lack of resolve, then seeming to yield to temp-
tation, he had, for safety's sake, explained to her that at
moments of elation he was subject to sundry angular
aches. So now he began gradually releasing her hand and,
rather crudely feigning twinges in his temple, said he was
going out for a breath of air. "You must understand," he
added, noticing the oddly intent gaze (or was he imagining
things?) of her two eyes and wart, "you must understand—happiness is so new to me ... and your closeness ... no, I never even dared dream of having such a
wife. ..."

"Just don't be long. I go to bed early, and don't like being awakened," she answered, letting down her freshly waved hair and tapping the top button of his waistcoat with her fingernail; then she gave him a little shove, and he realized that the invitation was not declinable.

Now he was roaming amid the shivering indigence of the November night, through the fog of streets that, ever since the Great Flood, had fallen into a state of perpetual damp. In an attempt to distract himself, he concentrated on his bookkeeping, his prisms, his profession, artificially magnifying its importance in his life—and it all kept dissolving in the mush, the feverish chill of the night, the agony of undulating lights. Yet, for the very reason that any kind of happiness was totally out of the question at the moment, something else suddenly became clear. He took precise measure of how far he had come, evaluated the entire instability and spectrality of his calculations, this whole quiet madness, the evident error of the obsession, which was free and genuine only when flowering within the confines of fantasy but which had now deviated from that sole legitimate form, to embark (with the pathetic diligence of a lunatic, a cripple, an obtuse child— yes, at any moment it would be rebuffed and thrashed!) on designs and actions that lay within the sole competence of adult, material life. And he could still get out of it! Flee immediately, then send a hurried letter to that person explaining that cohabitation was impossible for him (any reasons would do), that only a somewhat eccentric sense of compassion (expand) had motivated his commitment to support her, and that now, having legitimated it forever (be more specific), he was once again withdrawing into his fairyland obscurity.

"On the other hand," he continued mentally, under the impression that he was still pursuing the same sober line of reasoning (and not noticing that a banished barefoot creature had returned by the back door), "how simple it would be if dear Mummy were to die tomorrow. But no—she's in no hurry, she has sunk her teeth into life, and will hang on, and what do I stand to gain if she takes her time dying, and what arrives for her funeral will be a touch-me-not of sixteen or a stranger of twenty? How simple it would be" (he reflected, pausing, quite appropriately, by the illuminated display window of a pharmacy) "if there were some poison handy.... Certainly wouldn't need much, if, for her, a cup of chocolate is as deadly as strychnine! But a poisoner leaves his cigarette ash in the descended elevator.... Besides, they'll inevitably open her up, out of sheer habit." And even though reason and conscience vied with each other (all the while egging him on a little) in affirming that in any case, even if he were to find an untraceable poison, he was not one to commit murder (unless, perhaps, the poison were quite, quite untraceable, and even then—in the extreme hypothesis—for the sole purpose of curtailing the torments of a wife who was doomed, no matter what), he gave free rein to the theoretical development of an impossible thought as his absent gaze stumbled on impeccably packaged vials, the model of a liver, a panopticon of soaps, the reciprocal, splendidly coral-colored smiles of a feminine head and a masculine one gazing gratefully at each other. Then he slitted his eyes, cleared his throat, and, after a moment's hesitation, entered the pharmacy.

When he returned home it was dark in the apartment— the hope darted through his mind that she might already be asleep, but, alas, the door to her bedroom had been underlined with rulerlike precision by a fine-honed point of light.

"Charlatans...," he thought with a grim contortion. "We'll have to stick to the original version. I'll say good night to the dear departed and turn in." (What about tomorrow? What about the next day? What about all the days after that?)

But in the middle of his farewell speeches about his migraine, by her luxuriant headboard, things suddenly, unexpectedly, and spontaneously took a sharply angled turn and identity became immaterial, so that, after the fact, it was with astonishment that he discovered the corpse of the miraculously vanquished giantess and gazed at the moiré girdle that almost totally concealed her scar.

Of late she had been feeling tolerably well (the only complaint that still tormented her was eructation), but, during the very first days of their marriage, the pains she knew from the previous winter quietly reappeared. She posited, not unpoetically, that the massive, grouchy organ that had, as it were, dozed away "like an old dog" amid the warmth of incessant pampering was now jealous of her heart, a newcomer that "had been given but a single pat." Be that as it may, she spent a good month in bed listening intently to this internal turmoil, to the tentative scrabbling and the cautious nibbling; then it all quieted down, she even got up, rummaged through her first husband's letters, burned some of them, sorted certain exceedingly old small objects—a child's thimble; a mesh change purse of her mother's; something else, thin, golden, fluid as time itself. At Christmastime she again grew ill, and her daughter's planned visit came to nought.

He was unfailingly attentive. He made mooing sounds of consolation and accepted her awkward caresses with concealed hatred when, on occasion, she tried to explain, grimacing, that not she but *it* (a little finger indicated her belly) was responsible for their nocturnal separation, and it all sounded exactly as if she were pregnant (a false pregnancy, a pregnancy with her own death). Always even-tempered, always self-controlled, he sustained the smooth tone he had assumed from the start, and she was grateful for everything—for the old-fashioned gallantry with which he treated her, the polite form of address that in her estimation gave tenderness a dignified dimension, the way he satisfied her whims, the new radio phonograph, his docile acquiescence to twice changing the nurses who were hired to care for her around the clock.

On trifling errands, she would let him out of her sight no farther than to the corner room, while, when he went out on business, they jointly established beforehand the precise duration of his absence and, since his work did not call for a fixed schedule, on each occasion he had to battle—gaily, but with clenched teeth—for every grain of time. Impotent rage writhed inside him, the ashes of crumbling combinations stifled him, but he was sick of trying to hasten her demise; the very hope of it had become so vulgarized that he preferred to court its antithesis: perhaps by spring she would recover to such a degree that she would let him take the girl to the seashore for a few days. But how could he lay the groundwork? Originally he had imagined that it would be easy, sometime, under the guise of a business trip, to whip over to that town with its black church and its gardens reflected in the river; but when he once mentioned that, by a stroke of luck, he might be able to visit her daughter if he had to travel to a certain destination (he named a nearby city), he had the sensation that some vague, tiny, almost subconscious ember of jealousy had suddenly enlivened her hitherto nonexistent eyes. He hastily changed the subject, and contented himself with the thought that she herself apparently

had promptly forgotten that idiotic flash of intuition, which there was of course no point in reigniting.

The regularity of the fluctuations in her health seemed to him to embody the very mechanics of her existence; that regularity became the regularity of life itself; for his part, he noticed that his work, the precision of his eye, and the faceted transparency of his deductions had begun to suffer from the ceaseless vacillation of his soul between despair and hope, the perpetual ripple of unsatisfied desires, the painful burden of his rolled-up, tucked-away passion—the entire savage, stifling existence that he, and only he, had brought upon himself.

Sometimes he would walk past young girls at play, and sometimes a pretty one would catch his eye; but what that eye perceived was the senselessly smooth movement of slow-motion film, and he himself marveled at how unresponsive and occupied he was, how specifically the sensations recruited from every side—melancholy, avidity, tenderness, madness—were now concentrated upon the image of that absolutely unique and irreplaceable being who used to rush past with sun and shade contending for her dress. And sometimes, at night, when everything had quieted down—the radio phonograph, the water in the bathroom, the nurse's soft white footfalls, that endlessly protracted sound (worse than any bang) with which she closed the doors, the teaspoon's cautious tinkle, the click-click of the medicine cabinet, that person's distant, sepulchral lamentations—when it had all grown totally still, he would lie supine and evoke the one and only image, entwine his smiling victim with eight hands, which turned into eight tentacles affixed to every detail of her nudity, and at last he would dissolve in a black mist and lose her in the blackness, and the blackness spread everywhere, and was but the blackness of the night in his solitary bedroom.

IN SPRING THE ILLNESS seemed to take a turn for the worse; there was a consultation and she was transported to the hospital. There, on the eve of the operation, she spoke to him with sufficient clarity, in spite of her suffering, about the will, the attorney, what he must do in case tomorrow she ... She made him swear twice—yes, twice—that he would treat the girl as if he were her real ... And that he would see to it that she bore no ill feelings toward her late mother. "Maybe we should have her come after all," he said, louder than intended, "what do you think?" But she had already finished giving instructions, and tightly shut her eyes in agony; he stood for a while by the window, heaved a sigh, kissed the yellow fist on the folded-back sheet, and left.

Early the following morning he had a call from one of the doctors at the hospital, informing him that the operation had just ended, that it had apparently been a total success, surpassing the surgeon's every hope, but that it would be best not to visit until tomorrow.

"Success, eh? Total, eh?" he muttered incoherently, rushing from room to room, "Isn't that just dandy.... Congratulate us—we're going to convalesce, we're going to bloom.... What's going on here?" he abruptly cried in a guttural voice, giving the toilet door such a slam that the crystalware in the dining room reacted with fright. "We'll see about this," he continued amid the panic-stricken chairs, "Yes sirree...I'll show you a success! Success, suckercess." He mocked the pronunciation of sniveling fate. "Just nifty, isn't it. We'll keep on living and thriving, and marry off our daughter nice and early—no matter if she's a little frail, for the bridegroom will be a lusty fellow, he'll go ramming rough-shod into her frailty.... No, I've had enough of this! I've taken all the derision I'm going to! I too have a voice in the matter! I..."—and suddenly his roving rage happened upon an unexpected prey.

He froze, his fingers ceased twitching, his eyes rolled up for an instant—and he returned from this brief stupor with a smile. "I've had enough," he kept repeating, but with a different, almost propitiatory tone.

He immediately obtained the needed information: there was a most convenient express at 12:23, arriving at exactly 4:00 P.M. The return connection was not as simple . . . he would have to hire a car and leave immediately—by nightfall we'll be back here, the two of us, in utter seclusion, the little thing will be tired and sleepy, get your clothes off quick, I'll rock you to sleep—that's all, just some cosy cuddling, who wants to be sentenced to hard labor (although, incidentally, hard labor now would be better than some bastard in the future) . . . the stillness, her naked clavicles, the little straps, the buttons in back, the foxlike silk between her shoulder blades, her sleepy yawns, her hot armpit, her legs, her tenderness—mustn't lose my head . . . although what could be more natural than bringing home my little stepdaughter, deciding on it after all—they're cutting open her mother, aren't they? . . . Normal sense of responsibility, normal paternal zeal, besides, didn't the mother herself ask me to "take care of the girl"? And while the other is quietly reposing in the hospital, what—we repeat—what could be more natural if here, where my darling couldn't possibly disturb anybody . . . At the same time she'll be close by, one never knows, one must be ready for any eventuality. . . . A success, was it? All the better—their character improves as they convalesce, and if madam still elects to be angry, we'll explain, we'll explain, we wanted to do what was best, maybe we got a little flustered, we admit, but all with the best ...

In a joyful rush, he changed the sheets on his bed (in *her* former bedroom); tidied up summarily; bathed; called off a business meeting; canceled the char; had a quick snack in his "bachelor" restaurant; bought a supply of dates, ham, rye bread, whipped cream, muscat grapes— had he forgotten anything?—and, when he got home, disintegrated into multiple packages and kept visualizing how she would pass here and sit down there, springily bracing herself behind her back with her slender bare arms, all curly and dark—and at that moment there was a call from the hospital asking him to look in after all; on the way to the station he reluctantly stopped by and learned that the person was no more.

He was seized first of all by a sense of enraged disappointment: it meant that his plan had fallen through, that this night with all its warm, cosy closeness had been snatched from him, and that, when she arrived in response to a telegram, it would naturally be in the company of that hag and that hag's husband, and the two of them would settle in for a good week. But the very nature of this first reaction, the momentum of this shortsighted rush of emotion, created a vacuum, since an immediate transition from vexation at her death (which happened to have temporarily interfered) to gratitude (for the basic course destiny had taken) was impossible. Meanwhile, that vacuum was filling with preliminary, grayly human content. Sitting on a bench in the hospital garden, gradually calming down, preparing for the various steps of the funeral procedure, he mentally reviewed with appropriate sadness what he had just seen with his own eyes: the polished forehead, the translucent nostrils with the pearly wart on one side, the ebony cross, all of death's jewelry work. He parenthetically gave surgery a contemptuous dismissal and started thinking what a superb period she had had under his tutelage, how he had incidentally provided her with some real happiness to brighten the last days of her vegetative existence, and thence it was already a natural transition to crediting clever Fate with splendid behavior, and to the first delicious throb in his bloodstream: the lone wolf was getting ready to don Granny's nightcap.

He was expecting them next day at lunchtime. The doorbell rang on schedule, but the late person's friend stood on the doorstep alone (extending her bony hands and taking unfair advantage of a severe cold for the exigencies of obvious condolence): neither her husband nor "the little orphan" could come because both were laid up with the flu. His disappointment was alleviated by the thought that it was best this way—why spoil things? The girl's presence amid this combination of funereal encumbrances would have been just as agonizing as had been her arrival for the wedding, and it would be much more sensible to spend the coming days getting the formalities over with and thoroughly preparing a radical leap into complete safety. The only part that irritated him was the way the woman said "both"—the bond of illness (as if the two patients were sharing a common sickbed), the bond of contagion (maybe that vulgarian, following her up a steep staircase, liked to paw her bared thighs).

Feigning total shock—which was simplest of all, as murderers know too—he sat like a benumbed widower, his larger-than-life hands lowered, scarcely moving his lips in reply to her advice that he relieve the constipation of grief with tears, and watched with a turbid gaze as she blew her nose (all three were united by the cold— that was better). When, absently but greedily attacking the ham, she said such things as "At least her suffering did not last long" or "Thank God she was unconscious," on the lumped-together assumption that suffering and sleep were the natural human lot, that the worms had kind little faces, and that the supreme supine flotation took place in a blissful stratosphere, he nearly answered that death, as such, always had been and always would be an obscene idiot, but realized in time that this might cause his consoler to have disagreeable doubts about his ability to impart a religious and moral education to the adolescent girl.

There were very few people at the funeral (but for some

reason a friend of sorts from former times, a gold crafts-
man, showed up with his wife), and later, in the home-
bound car, a plump lady (who had also been at his farcical
wedding) told him, compassionately but in no uncertain
terms (as his bowed head bobbed with the car's motion),
that now, at least, something must be done about the
child's abnormal situation (meanwhile his late spouse's
friend pretended to gaze out into the street), and that
paternal concerns would undoubtedly give him the needed
consolation, and a third woman (an infinitely remote relative of the deceased) joined in, saying, "And what a pretty
girl she is! You'll have to watch her like a hawk—she's
already biggish for her age, just wait another three years
and the boys will be sticking to her like flies, you'll have
no end of worries," and meanwhile he was guffawing
and guffawing to himself, floating on featherbeds of happiness.

The day before, in response to a second telegram ("Wor-
ried how is your health kiss"—and this kiss written on
the telegraph blank was the first real one), came the news
that neither of them had any more fever, and, before
leaving for home, the still runny-nosed friend showed
him a small box and asked if she could take it for the
girl (it contained some maternal trinkets from the remote,
sacred past), after which she inquired what would happen
next, and how. Only then, speaking extremely slowly and
expressionlessly, with frequent pauses, as though with

every syllable he were overcoming the speechlessness of sorrow, he announced to her what would happen and how: after first thanking her for the year of care, he advised her that in exactly two weeks he would come to fetch his daughter (the very word he used) to take her south and then probably abroad. "Yes, that's wise," replied the other with relief (somewhat tempered, but only by the thought, he hoped, that, of late, she had probably been making a nice little profit on her ward). "Go away, distract yourself—there's nothing like a trip to calm one's grief."

He needed those two weeks to organize his affairs so he would not have to think about them for at least a year; then he would see. He was forced to sell certain items from his own collection. And while packing he happened to find in his desk a coin he had once picked up (which, incidentally, had turned out to be counterfeit). He chuckled: the talisman had already done its job.

WHEN HE BOARDED THE TRAIN, day-after-tomorrow's address still seemed a shoreline in a torrid mist, a preliminary symbol of future anonymity. The only thing he tentatively planned was where they would pass the night on the way to that shimmering South; he found it unnecessary to predetermine subsequent habitations. The locus did not matter—it would always be adorned by a little naked foot; the destination was immaterial—as long as he could abscond with her into the azure void. The telegraph poles, like violin bridges, flew past with spasms of guttural music. The throbbing of the car's partitions was like the crackle of mightily bulging wings. We shall live far away, now in the hills, now by the sea, in a hothouse warmth where savagelike nudity will automatically become habitual, perfectly alone (no servants!), seeing no one, just the two of us in an eternal nursery, and thus any remaining sense of shame will be dealt its final blow. There will be constant merriment, pranks, morning kisses, tussles on the shared bed, a single, huge sponge shedding its tears on four shoulders, squirting with laughter amid four legs.

Luxuriating in the concentrated rays of an internal sun, he pondered the delicious alliance between premeditation and pure chance, the Edenic discoveries that awaited her, the way the amusing traits peculiar to bodies of different sex, seen at close range, would appear extraordinary yet natural and homey to her, while the subtle distinctions of intricately refined passion would long remain for her but the alphabet of innocent caresses: she would be entertained only with storybook images (the pet giant, the fairy-tale forest, the sack wih its treasure), and with the amusing consequences that would ensue when she inquisitively fingered the toy with the familiar but never tedious trick. He was convinced that, as long as novelty still prevailed and she did not look around her, it would be easy, by means of pet names and jokes confirming the essentially aimless simplicity of given oddities, to divert a normal girl's attention ahead of time from the comparisons, generalizations, and questions that might be prompted by something overheard previously, or a dream, or her first menstruation, so as to prepare a painless transition from a world of semiabstractions of which she was probably semi-conscious (such as the correct interpretation of a neighbor's autonomously swelling belly, or schoolgirl predilections for the mug of a matinee idol), from everything in any way connected with adult love, into the reality of pleasant fun, while decorum and morality, aware neither of the goings-on nor of the address, would refrain from visiting.

Raising drawbridges might be an effective system of protection until such time as the flowering chasm itself reached up to the chamber with a robust young branch. Yet, precisely because during the first two years or so the captive would be ignorant of the temporarily noxious nexus between the puppet in her hands and the puppet-master's panting, between the plum in her mouth and the rapture of the distant tree, he would have to be particularly cautious, not to let her go anywhere alone, make frequent changes of domicile (the ideal would be a mini-villa in a blind garden), keep a sharp eye out lest she make friends with other children or have occasion to start chatting with the woman from the greengrocer's or the char, for there was no telling what impudent elf might fly from the lips of enchanted innocence—and what monster a stranger's ear would carry off for examination and discussion by the sages. And yet, for what could one possibly reproach the enchanter?

He knew he would find sufficient delights in her so as not to disenchant her prematurely, emphasize anything about her by unduly obvious manifestations of rapture, or push his way too insistently into some little blind alley as he acted out his monastic promenade. He knew he would make no attempt on her virginity in the tightest and pinkest sense of the term until the evolution of their caresses had ascended a certain invisible step. He would hold back until that morning when, still laughing, she would hearken to her own responsiveness and, growing mute, demand that the search for the hidden musical string be made jointly.

As he imagined the coming years, he continued to envision her as an adolescent—such was the carnal postulate. However, catching himself on this premise, he realized without difficulty that, even if the putative passage of time contradicted, for the moment, a permanent foundation for his feelings, the gradual progression of successive delights would assure natural renewals of his pact with happiness, which took into account, as well, the adaptability of living love. Against the light of that happiness, no matter what age she attained—seventeen, twenty—her present image would always transpire through her metamorphoses, nourishing their translucent strata from its internal fountainhead. And this very process would allow him, with no loss or diminishment, to savor each unblemished stage of her transformations. Besides, she herself, delineated and elongated into womanhood, would never again be free to dissociate, in her consciousness and her memory, her own development from that of their love, her childhood recollections from her recollections of male tenderness. Consequently, past, present, and future would appear to her as a single radiance whose source had emanated, as she had herself, from him, from her viviparous lover.

Thus they would live on—laughing, reading books, marveling at gilded fireflies, talking of the flowering walled prison of the world, and he would tell her tales and she would listen, his little Cordelia, and nearby the sea would breathe beneath the moon. . . . And exceedingly slowly, at first with all the sensitivity of his lips, then in earnest, with all their weight, ever deeper, only thus—for the first time—into your inflamed heart, thus, forcing my way, thus, plunging into it, between its melting edges . . .

The lady who had been sitting across from him for some reason suddenly got up and went into another compartment; he glanced at the blank face of his wristwatch— it wouldn't be long now—and then he was already ascending next to a white wall crowned with blinding shards of glass as a multitude of swallows flew overhead.

He was met on the porch by the late person's friend, who explained the presence of a heap of ashes and charred logs in a corner of the garden by the fact that there had been a fire that night; the firemen had had trouble bringing the raging flames under control, had broken a young apple tree, and of course nobody had gotten any sleep. Just then *she* came out, in a dark knit dress (in this heat!) with a shiny leather belt, and a chain on her neck, wearing long black stockings, the poor thing, and at this very first instant he had the impression that she was not quite as pretty as before, that she had grown more snub-nosed and leggier. Gloomily, rapidly, with nothing but a feeling of acute tenderness for her mourning, he took her by the shoulder and kissed her warm hair.

"Everything could have caught fire!" she exclaimed, raising her rosily illumined face and goggling her eyes, in which shimmered the liquidly transparent reflections of sun and garden.

She contentedly held onto his arm as they entered the house behind its loudly talking mistress—and the spontaneity had already evaporated, already he was awkwardly bending his arm (or was it hers?)—and, at the door to the parlor, where resounded the monologue that had preceded them accompanied by the opening of shutters, he freed his hand and, feigning an absentminded caress (but actually totally engrossed for an instant in a good, firm feel, complete with dimple), he patted her on the hip— as if to say, run along, child—and then he was already sitting down, finding a place for his walking stick, lighting up, looking for an ashtray, saying something in answer to a question, filled all the while with a savage exultation.

He refused tea, explaining that at any moment the car he had ordered at the station would arrive, that it already contained his luggage (this detail, as occurs in dreams, had a certain glimmer of meaning), and that "you and I will be off to the seashore"—which he almost shouted in the direction of the girl who, turning in mid-step, nearly crashed into a stool, but instantly regained her youthful balance, turned, and sat down, covering the stool with her settling skirt.

"What?" she asked, brushing back her hair with a sidewise glance at the hostess (the stool had already once been broken). He said it again. She joyously raised her eyebrows—she had no idea it would happen like this, today.

"And I was hoping," lied the hostess, "that you would spend the night with us."

"Oh, no!" cried the girl, rushing over to him with a parquet slide, and then continued with unexpected rapidity, "Do you think I can learn how to swim soon? A friend of mine says you can, right away, all you have to do is learn not to be afraid first, and that takes a month. . . ." But the woman was already nudging her by the elbow so she would go finish packing, with Maria, the things that had been laid out in the left section of the wardrobe.

"I confess I don't envy you," she said, turning over her

77

tutelage, after the child had run out. "Lately, especially after her flu, she's been having all kinds of outbursts and tantrums; the other day she was rude to me—it's a difficult age. All in all I think it would be a good thing if you hired some young woman to look after her and, in the fall, found her a good Catholic boarding school. As you can see, the death of her mother has not been too much of a shock to her—of course, she may be holding it in, for all I know. Our shared existence is over with. . . . By the way, I still owe you . . . No, no, I won't hear of it, I insist. . . . Oh, he doesn't get home from work till around seven—he'll be very disappointed. . . . That's life, what can you do. At least she has found her peace in Heaven, poor thing, and you are looking better too. . . . If it hadn't been for our encounter . . . I simply don't see how I could have kept supporting someone else's child, and as for orphanages, they lead directly you know where. That's why I always say—you never know in life. Remember that day, on the bench—remember? It never occurred to me she could find a second husband, and yet my feminine intuition told me that something in you was longing for just that kind of refuge."

A car materialized behind the foliage. In we get! The familiar black cap, coat over her arm, a small suitcase, help from red-handed Maria. Just wait, you'll see the things I'll buy for you. . . . She insisted on sitting next to the driver, and he had to consent, concealing his chagrin.

The woman, whom we shall never see again, was waving good-bye with an apple-tree branch. Maria was shooing the chicks in. We're off, we're off.

He sat leaning back, holding his stick—a very valuable, antique thing with a thick coral head—between his legs, gazing through the glass partition at the beret and the contented shoulders. The weather was exceptionally warm for June, a stream of heat rushed in through the window, and soon he took off his tie and unbuttoned his collar.

After an hour the girl looked around at him (she was pointing at something beside the road but, although he turned, open-mouthed, he was too late to see anything— and, for some reason, with no logical connection, the thought crossed his mind that there was, after all, an age difference of nearly thirty years). At six they stopped for ice cream, while the talkative chauffeur drank beer at the next table, sharing various considerations with his client.

On we go. He looked at the forest that kept approaching in undulating hops from hillside to hillside until it slid down an incline and tripped over the road, where it was counted and stored away. "Shall we take a break here?" he wondered. "We could have a short walk, sit for a while on the moss among the mushrooms and the butter-flies. . . ." But he could not bring himself to stop the chauf-feur: there was something unbearable about the idea of a suspicious car standing idle on the highway.

Then it got dark and their headlights imperceptibly came on. They stopped for dinner at the first roadside eatery, the philosophizer again sprawled nearby, and seemed to be glancing over less at his employer's steak and potato croquettes than at the profile of the hair screening her face and at her exquisite cheek.... My darling is tired and flushed from the trip, the rich meat course, the drop of wine. The sleepless night with the rosy glow of the fire in the darkness is taking its toll, her napkin is slipping off the soft hollow of her skirt.... And now all this is mine.... He asked if they had rooms available—no, they did not.

In spite of her increasing lassitude she resolutely refused to exchange her seat in front for support in the car's cosy depths, saying she would get carsick in back. At last, at last, lights began ripening and bursting amid the hot, black void, a hotel was immediately selected and the agonizing journey paid for, and that part was done with. She was half asleep as she crawled out onto the sidewalk, halting numbly amid the bluish, coarse-grained darkness, the warm burnt fragrance, the roar and throb of two, three, four trucks taking advantage of the deserted nighttime street to descend with appalling speed from behind a bend that concealed a whining, straining, grinding upgrade.

A short-legged, macrocephalous old fellow in an unbuttoned waistcoat—sluggish, dawdling, explaining at

length and with guilty benevolence that he was only standing in for the owner who was his eldest son and who had
had to leave to attend to family matters—searched for a
long time in a black book, then announced that he did
not have a free room with twin beds (there was a flower
show in town, and many visitors) but that there was one
with a double bed, "which amounts to the same thing,
you and your daughter will be even more—" "All right,
all right," interrupted the traveler, as the hazy child stood
off by herself, blinking and trying to focus her languishing
gaze on a doubling cat.

They headed upstairs. The help apparently went to bed
early, or else they were absent too. Meanwhile, the stooping, groaning gnome tried one key after another; an old
woman with curly gray hair, in azure pajamas, her face
tanned to a nutlike hue, emerged from the toilet next
door with an admiring glance at this tired, pretty girl in
the obedient pose of tender victim, whose dark dress stood
out against the ocher of the wall where she leaned her
shoulderblades, her tousled head thrown slightly back and
slowly turning from side to side, and her eyelids twitching
as though she were trying to unravel her excessively thick
lashes. "Come on, get it open," irritably said her father,
a balding gentleman, also a tourist.

"Is this where I'm going to sleep?" the girl asked in-
differently, and when, struggling with the shutters,
squeezing tight their eyelike chinks, he replied affirma-

81

tively, she took a look at the cap she was holding and limply tossed it on the wide bed.

"There we are," said he after the old man had dragged in their suitcases and left, and there remained in the room only the pounding of his heart and the distant throbbing of the night. "There, now it's time for bed."

Reeling with sleepiness, she bumped into the corner of an armchair, at which point he, simultaneously sitting down in it, took her by the hip and drew her close. She straightened, stretching up like an angel, for a split second tensed every muscle, took another half step, and softly descended onto his lap. "My sweetheart, my poor little girl," he spoke in a kind of general mist of pity, tenderness, and desire, as he observed her drowsiness, her wooziness, her diminishing smile, palpating her through the dark dress, feeling, through the thin wool, the band of the orphan's garter on her bare skin, thinking how defenseless, abandoned, warm she was, reveling in the animate weight of her legs as they slithered apart and then, with the faintest corporeal rustle, recrossed at a slightly higher level. She slowly entwined a somnolent arm, in its snug little sleeve, around his nape, engulfing him with the chestnut fragrance of her soft hair, but her arm slid down, and she sleepily nudged with the sole of her sandal the bag standing next to the armchair.... A rumbling approached and receded beyond the window. Then, in the silence, the whine of a mosquito became audible, and for some reason it evoked a fleeting memory of something infinitely remote, late bedtimes in his childhood, a dissolving lamp, the hair of his sister, his coeval, who had died long, long ago. "My sweetheart," he repeated, and, nuzzling a curl out of the way, cuddling mussily, he tasted, exerting almost no pressure, her hot silky neck near the chill of the chain; then, taking her by the temples so that her eyes lengthened and narrowed, he began kissing her parting lips, her teeth. . . . She slowly wiped her mouth with bent knuckles, her head collapsed onto his shoulder, and between her eyelids there showed only a narrow, sunset-hued luster, for she was virtually asleep.

There was a knock at the door. He gave a violent start (hurriedly withdrawing his hand from her belt without having figured out how to unhook it). "Wake up, get off," he said, giving her a quick shake. She opened her vacant eyes wide and slithered down over the hummock of his knee. "Come in," he said.

The old fellow peeked in and announced that the gentleman was wanted downstairs, that there was somebody from the police station to see him.

"The police?" he asked, grimacing with bewilderment. "The police? . . . All right, you can go—I'll be right down," he added without getting up. He lit a cigarette, blew his nose and carefully refolded his handkerchief, squinting through the smoke. "Listen," he said before going out, "your bag is over here. I'll open it for you and you take out whatever you need, get undressed and go to bed in the meantime. The bathroom is the first door on the left."

"Why the police?" he thought as he descended the badly lit staircase. "What do they want?"

"What's the matter?" he asked sharply upon reaching the entrance hall and seeing an already restless gendarme, a swarthy giant with a cretin's eyes and chin.

"The matter," came the willing answer, "is that apparently you'll have to accompany me to the police station—it's not far."

"Near or far," spoke the traveler after a brief pause, "it's after midnight, and I was getting ready for bed. Moreover, please be advised that any deduction, especially such a dynamic one, is a cry in the woods to an ear unfamiliar with the previous train of thought, or, to put it more simply, what is logical gets construed as being zoological. Besides, a globetrotter freshly and for the first time arrived in your hospitable little town would be curious to know your basis—some local custom, perhaps— for selecting the middle of the night to extend an invitation, an invitation that is all the more unacceptable because I am not alone but have a weary little girl with me. No, wait, I'm not through yet.... Who ever heard of justice putting the enforcement of a law first and the grounds for its application second? Wait for some accusations, gentlemen, wait for somebody to lodge a little complaint! For the time being, my neighbor cannot see through the wall, and the chauffeur cannot scrutinize my soul. In conclusion—and perhaps most important—be so kind as to acquaint yourself with my papers."

The now befuddled dimwit acquainted himself, came to his senses, and went to work on the unlucky old man. It turned out that the latter not only had confused two similar names, but was unable to explain when and for what destination the desired drifter had departed.

"All right, all right," said the traveler peaceably, having vented his vexation for the delay entirely on his too hasty foe, and fully aware of his own invulnerability (thank Doom she did not sit in the back of the car; thank Doom they did not go mushroom-hunting in the June sun— and, of course, that the shutters were tight).

Reaching the landing at a run, he realized he had not noted the room number, paused in hesitation, spat out the butt of his cigarette. . . . Now, however, the impatience of his emotions kept him from going back down for information, and besides it was unnecessary—he recalled the arrangement of the doors in the corridor. He found the right door, licked his chops, grabbed the doorknob, was about to—

The door was locked; he felt a horrid pang in the pit of his stomach. If she had locked herself in, it was to keep him out, it meant she was suspicious. . . . Shouldn't have kissed her like that . . . Must have frightened her off, or she may have noticed something . . . Or the reason was sillier and simpler: she had naively decided that he had gone to bed in another room, it had not even entered her mind that she would be sleeping in the same room with a stranger—yes, still a stranger. And he knocked, as yet scarcely aware himself of the intensity of his alarm and irritation.

He heard some abrupt female laughter, the repulsive exclamation of bedsprings, and then the slap-slap of bare feet. "Who is it?" asked an angry male voice. . . . "Wrong room, eh? Well, next time please find the right room. There's somebody in here hard at work, there's somebody in here trying to train a young person, that somebody is being interrupted. . . ." Another burst of laughter resounded in the background.

A vulgar mistake, nothing more. He continued along the corridor—and suddenly realized he was on the wrong landing. He retraced his steps, turned the corner, cast a puzzled look at a meter on the wall, at a sink beneath a dripping faucet, at somebody's tan shoes outside a door, turned again—the staircase had vanished! The one he finally found turned out to be different: he went down only to lose his way in some faintly lit storage rooms where stood trunks and, from the corners, now a cabinet, now a vacuum cleaner, now a broken stool, now the skeleton of a bed protruded with an air of fatality. He swore under his breath, losing control, exasperated by these obstacles. . . . At last he reached a door and gave it

a shove, banged his head on a low lintel, and ducked out
into the entrance hall next to a dimly illuminated nook,
where, scratching the bristles of his cheek, the old man
was peering into his black book, and the gendarme snored
on a bench next to him—every bit as in a guardroom.
Getting the needed information was a matter of one minute, slightly prolonged by the old man's apologies.

He went in. He went in and first of all, before he looked
at anything, stooping furtively, turned the key twice in
the lock. Then he saw the black stocking with its elastic
under the washstand. Then he saw the opened suitcase
containing an incipient disorder, and a waffle-textured
towel half extracted by its ear. Then he saw the dress and
underwear heaped on the armchair, the belt, the other
stocking. Only then did he turn toward the island of the
bed.

She was lying supine atop the undisturbed blanket, with
her left arm behind her head, in her little robe, whose
lower part had fallen open—she had not been able to
find her nightgown—and, by the light of the reddish
lampshade, through the haze and stuffiness of the room,
he could see her narrow, concave belly between the innocent, projecting hipbones. With the roar of cannon fire
a truck ascended from the bottom of the night, a glass
tinkled on the marble top of the night table, and it was
strange to see how her enchanted slumber flowed evenly
past everything.

Tomorrow of course we'll begin at the beginning with a carefully pondered progression, but for now you're asleep, you're extraneous, don't interfere with grown-ups, this is how it must be, it's my night, it's my business. He undressed, lay down to the left of the captive, rocking her ever so slightly, and froze, cautiously catching his breath. So. The hour he had deliriously desired for a full quarter century had finally come, yet it was shackled, even cooled by the cloud of his bliss. The flow and ebb of her light-colored robe, mingling with revelations of her beauty, still quivered before his eyes, intricately rippled as if seen through cut glass. He simply could not find the focal point of happiness, did not know where to begin, what one could touch, and how, within the realm of her repose, in order to savor this hour to the fullest. So. To start with, proceeding with clinical caution, he removed from his wrist the walleye of time and, reaching over her head, placed it on the bedside table between a glistening drop of water and the empty glass.

So. A priceless original: sleeping girl, oil. Her face in its soft nest of curls, scattered here, wadded together there, with those little fissures on her parched lips, and that special crease in the eyelids over the barely joined lashes, had a russet, roseate tint where the lighted cheek—whose Florentine outline was a smile in itself—showed through. Sleep, my precious, don't listen to me.

Already his gaze (the self-aware gaze of one who is

observing an execution or a point at the bottom of an abyss) was creeping downward along her form and his left hand was in motion—but here he gave a start as if someone had moved in the room, at the edge of his field of vision, for he had not immediately recognized the reflection in the wardrobe mirror (his pajama stripes, receding into the shadow, and an indistinct glint on the lacquered wood, and something black under her pink ankle).

Finally making up his mind, he gently stroked her long, just slightly parted, faintly sticky legs, which grew cooler and a little coarser on the way down, and progressively warmer farther up. He recalled, with a furious sense of triumph, the roller skates, the sun, the chestnut trees, everything—while he kept stroking with his fingertips, trembling and casting sidelong looks at the plump promontory, with its brand-new downiness, which, independently but with a familial parallel, embodied a concentrated echo of something about her lips and cheeks. A little higher, at the translucent bifurcation of a vein, the mosquito was hard at work. He jealously shooed it away, inadvertently contributing to the fall of a flap that had long been in the way, and there they were, those strange, sightless little breasts, swollen with what seemed two tender abscesses, and now a thin, still childlike muscle was bared, and next to it the stretched, milk-white hollow of her armpit with five or six diverging, silky-dark streaks, and down there, too, obliquely flowed the golden little stream of chain (with a cross, probably, or a charm at its end), and then once again there was cotton—the sleeve of her sharply thrown-back arm.

Yet another truck hurtled past, howling and filling the room with a tremor. He paused in his perlustration, leaning awkwardly over her, involuntarily pressing into her with his gaze, feeling the adolescent scent of her skin mingle with that of the russet hair and penetrate his blood like a gnawing itch. What am I to do with you, what am I to—

The girl heaved a sigh in her sleep, opening her tightly shut navel like an eye, then slowly, with a cooing moan, breathed out, and that was all she needed to glide on in her previous torpor. He carefully pulled the crushed black cap out from under her heel and froze again, his temples throbbing, the ache of his tension pounding. He dared not kiss those angular nipples, those long toes with their yellowish nails. His eyes returned from everywhere else to converge on the same suedelike fissure, which somehow seemed to come alive under his prismatic stare. He still did not know what to undertake, afraid of missing something, of not taking full advantage of the fairy-tale firmness of her sleep.

The stuffy air and his excitement were growing unbearable. He slightly loosened his pajama drawstring, which had been cutting into his belly, and a tendon emitted a squeak as his lips almost incorporeally brushed the spot where a birthmark was visible beneath her rib. . . . But he was uncomfortable and hot, and the congestion of his blood demanded the impossible. Then, starting little by little to cast his spell, he began passing his magic wand above her body, almost touching the skin, torturing himself with her attraction, her visible proximity, the fantastic confrontation permitted by the slumber of this naked girl, whom he was measuring, as it were, with an enchanted yardstick—until she made a faint motion, and turned her face away with a barely audible, somnolent smack of her lips. Everything again froze still, and now, amid her brown locks, he could make out the crimson border of her ear and the palm of her liberated hand, forgotten in its previous position. Onward, onward. In parenthetical flashes of consciousness, as though on the verge of oblivion, he had fleeting glimpses of incidental ephemera—some bridge over speeding railway cars, an air bubble in the glass of some window, the dented fender of a car, some other object, a waffle-patterned towel seen somewhere not long ago—and meanwhile, slowly, with baited breath, he was inching closer and then, coordinating all his movements, he began molding himself to her, testing the fit. . . . A spring apprehensively yielded under his side; his right elbow, cautiously cracking, sought a support; his sight was clouded by a secret concentration. . . . He felt the flame of her shapely thigh, felt that he could restrain himself no longer, that nothing mattered now, and, as the sweetness came to a boil between his woolly tufts and her hip, how joyously his life was emancipated and reduced to the simplicity of paradise—and having barely had time still to think, "No, I beg you, don't take it away!" he saw that she was fully awake and looking wild-eyed at his rearing nudity.

For an instant, in the hiatus of a syncope, he also saw how it appeared to her: some monstrosity, some ghastly disease—or else she already knew, or it was all of that together. She was looking and screaming, but the enchanter did not yet hear her screams; he was deafened by his own horror, kneeling, catching at the folds, snatching at the drawstring, trying to stop it, hide it, snapping with his oblique spasm, as senseless as pounding in place of music, senselessly discharging molten wax, too late to stop it or conceal it. How she rolled from the bed, how she was shrieking now, how the lamp scampered off in its red cowl, what a thundering came from outside the window, shattering, destroying the night, demolishing everything, everything. . . . "Be quiet, it's nothing bad, it's just a kind of game, it happens sometimes, just be quiet," he implored, middle-aged and sweaty, covering himself with a raincoat he had glimpsed in passing, shuddering, donning it, missing the armhole. Like a child in a screen drama, she shielded herself with her sharp little elbow, tearing from his grasp and still yelling senselessly, and somebody was pounding on the wall, demanding inconceivable silence. She tried to run out of the room, could not unlock the door, he could not catch hold of anything or anyone, she was growing lighter, becoming slippery as a purple-buttocked foundling, with a distorted infant's face, scuttling from the threshold to the crib and crawling backward from the crib into the womb of a tempestuously resurrected mother. "I'll make you quiet down!" he was shouting (to a spasm, to the dotlike final drop, to nothingness). "All right, I'll leave, I'll make you—" He overcame the door, rushed out, deafeningly locked it behind him, and, still listening, gripping the key in his palm, barefoot and with a cold smear beneath his raincoat, stood where he was, gradually sinking.

But from a nearby room there had already appeared two robed old women; one of them—thickset, resembling a white-haired negro, wearing azure pajama bottoms, with the breathless, jerky cadence of a distant continent, suggesting animal defense leagues and women's clubs— was giving orders (at-once, *entlassen, et-tout-de-suite!*) and, clawing at the palm of his hand, nimbly knocked the key to the floor. For several elastic seconds he and she had a hip-shoving match, but in any event it was all over; heads emerged from every direction, a bell was clanging somewhere, behind a door a melodious voice seemed to be finishing a nursery tale (Mr. White-Tooth in the bed, the hoodlum brothers with their little red rifles), the old woman conquered the key, he gave her a quick swat on the cheek, and, with his whole body ringing, went running down the sticky steps. Toward him briskly clambered a dark-haired fellow with a goatee, clad only in underpants; after him wriggled a puny harlot. He rushed past them. Farther down came a specter in tan shoes, farther still the old man climbed bow-legged, followed by the avid gendarme. Past them. Leaving behind a multitude of synchronized arms extended over the banister in a splashlike gesture of invitation, he pirouetted into the street, for all was over, and it was imperative, by any stratagem, by any spasm, to get rid of the no-longer-needed, already-looked-at, idiotic world, on whose final page stood a lonely streetlamp with a shaded-out cat at its base. Already interpreting his sensation of barefootedness as a plunge into another element, he rushed off along the ashen sidewalk, pursued by the pounding footfalls of his already outdistanced heart. His desperate need for a torrent, a precipice, a railroad track—no matter what, but instantly—made him appeal for the very last time to the topography of his past. And when, in front of him, a grinding whine came from behind the hump of the side street, swelling to full growth when it had overcome the grade, distending the night, already illuminating the descent with two ovals of yellowish light, about to hurtle downward—then, as if it were a dance, as if the ripple of that dance had carried him to stage center, under this growing, grinning, megathundering mass, his partner in a crashing cracovienne, this thundering iron thing, this instantaneous cinema of dismemberment—that's it, drag me under, tear at my frailty— I'm traveling flattened, on my smacked-down face—hey, you're spinning me, don't rip me to pieces—you're shredding me, I've had enough. . . . Zigzag gymnastics of lightning, spectrogram of a thunderbolt's split seconds—and the film of life had burst.

On a Book Entitled The Enchanter

by Dmitri Nabokov

THE TITLE FOR THE FOLLOWING brief notes, which may interest the reader and perhaps answer a few questions, was chosen with the half-serious thought that a small echo of Father's postface to *Lolita* may amuse his shade wherever it may be.

In both translation and commentary I have tried hard to stick to the Nabokov rules: precision, artistic fidelity, no padding, no ascribing. Any conjecture beyond what I have ventured would violate those rules.

The translation itself reflects my intent to be faithful to VN in both the general and the specific, textual, senses.

Many years of translating for and with Father instilled in me those categorical requirements of his. The only cases where he considered departures admissable were untranslatable expressions and revisions of the text itself, in the translated version, by the original author. It is possible that VN, were he alive, might have exercised his authorial license to change certain details of *The Enchanter;* I believe, though, that he would have chosen to leave intact this model of conciseness and multilevel meaning. The rare instances where I have taken the liberty of making minor adjustments occur precisely where the technique—as in the telescoped Little Red Riding Hood wordplays (p. 67, l. 16; p. 93, l. 26) or the high-speed imagery of the finale—would have made a totally literal rendering meaningless in English. Elsewhere, on occasion, the English may seem simply a bit unorthodox. But so, in such cases, is the Russian.

Other possible translations of the Russian word *volshebnik* are "magician" or "conjuror," but I have respected Nabokov's express intention that, in this case, it be rendered as "enchanter." *Volshebnik* was written during October and November of 1939. It was signed "V. Sirin," a pseudonym that VN used for his Russian writings from his early youth on so that they would not be confused with those of his father, who had the same given name. *Sirin* in Russian is both a species of owl and a bird of ancient fable, but most probably has no connection, as some have suggested, with the word *siren*.

The original text was dictated to and typed by Father's first reader, Véra Nabokov. According to Nabokov's letters, he showed it shortly thereafter to four other people, literary friends of his (see Author's Note One).

At some point, apparently, a typescript was also shown to the émigré critic Vladimir Weidle, in Paris. It could not have been later than May 1940, when we sailed for New York. Andrew Field, who, it seems, read an article written nearly forty years after the fact by a very old Weidle not long before his death, claims[1] the piece shown to Weidle differed in several respects from *The Enchanter* (of which Field has a very sketchy idea at best, having seen only two pages and one or perhaps both of Nabokov's references presented at the beginning of this volume).

Presumably that version was called "The Satyr," the girl "was no more than ten," and the concluding scene was set not on the French Riviera but "in a remote little hotel in Switzerland." Field also attributes the name Arthur to the protagonist. It is unclear whether he got that from Weidle too, but more likely he simply gleaned it from Father's recollection in his postface to *Lolita*. I have suggested that Nabokov had thought of his protagonist as "Arthur," or perhaps even used that name in a preliminary draft. It is highly unlikely, however, that the name

[1] In *VN:The Art and Life of Vladimir Nabokov,* New York, Crown, 1986. An odd concoction of rancor, adulation, innuendo, and outright factual error, which I had occasion to read in page proof.

appeared in a manuscript "already marked with instructions for the printer," as Field has Weidle affirm.

As for the three differences Field cites, if his paraphrase of the Weidle article is accurate, then Weidle's memory of that distant event must have been a bit hazy (Field does admit, in fact, that Weidle "could not remember whether the girl is named in the story"). The fact is that there never was a version called "The Satyr"; indeed, such a title would seem most implausible to anyone with a sensitive ear for Nabokov's use of language. And I would attribute the same degree of credibility to the rest of Weidle's assertions.

I was five when *The Enchanter* was being written and was, if anything, a disruptive influence in our Paris apartment and our Riviera pensions. I recall that, between generous periods of play with me, Father would sometimes withdraw into the bathroom of our meager quarters to work in peace, although not, as John Shade does for shaving purposes in *Pale Fire,* on a board placed across the tub. While I was already aware that my father was a "writer," I had no idea of what was being written, and my parents certainly made no attempt to familiarize me with the story of *Volshebnik* (I think the only work of Father's I knew at the time was his Russian translation of *Alice in Wonderland* and the little tales and ditties he would improvise for me). It is possible that, when Father was writing *Volshebnik,* I had already been bundled off to Deauville with a cousin of Mother's, since it was feared that the rumble of Hitler's bombs might reach Paris. (It did, but only after our departure for America, and I think one of the few bombs actually dropped on the city did hit our building as we were crossing on the *Champlain.* The vessel, too, was destined to be destroyed after having safely delivered us with no more than the spout of an occasional whale to alarm a couple of trigger-happy gunners; on its next voyage, for which we had originally held passage, it was sunk with all aboard by a German submarine.)

Other than what already is or will now become publicly available, neither Mother nor I can reconstruct much about the birth of the idea in VN's mind, but can only alert the reader to some of the inane hypotheses that have been propounded, especially of late. As for the link with *Lolita,* the theme had probably lain dormant (as Nabokov suggests in "On a Book Entitled *Lolita*") until the new novel began germinating, somewhat as in the case of the interrupted *Solus Rex* and the later, very different, but nonetheless related *Pale Fire.*

It is clear from Nabokov's postface to *Lolita,* originally written in 1956, that, at the time, he believed whatever copies had existed of the *Volshebnik* typescript had been destroyed, and his recollection of the novella was somewhat blurred, partly by the passing of time, but mainly by his rejection of it as "a dead scrap," superseded by

Lolita. The surviving text probably turned up not long before he proposed it, with reborn enthusiasm, to G. P. Putnam's Sons (see Author's Note Two).

I became aware of the work's existence quite late and in rather a vague way, and had occasion to read it only in the early eighties, when our voluminous archives were finally organized by Brian Boyd (the author of a proper literary biography of VN, to be published in 1988). It was then that *Volshebnik*, which had been consulted by Father in the sixties before it submerged anew among the jumble of belongings that had been shipped to Switzerland from an Ithaca warehouse, resurfaced.

I completed a more or less final draft of the translation in September of 1985.

For the initial impetus to attack what was not an easy job I must give heartfelt thanks to Matthew Bruccoli, who had envisioned a very limited edition of the work, as Nabokov had originally suggested to Walter Minton, then president of Putnam.

The timing of this public debut of *The Enchanter* is not without an amusing and instructive coincidental sidelight. In 1985, in Paris, there began an energetic one-man campaign to attribute to Vladimir Nabokov a pseudonymous, quite un-Nabokovian book from the mid-thirties entitled *Novel with Cocaine*.

Falling as it does within the very limited realm of

rediscovered Nabokoviana, *The Enchanter* is a most appropriate example of the strikingly original prose Nabokov-Sirin produced in his most mature—and final—years as a novelist in his mother tongue (not long before writing *The Enchanter* in 1939, in fact, he had completed his first major English work, *The Real Life of Sebastian Knight,* and 1940 was to be the year of our transplantation to the United States).

For anyone who may harbor lingering doubts about the authorship of the other book, a quick comparison of its substance and style with those of *The Enchanter* should suffice to put the final round of shot into this moribund canard.

A brief account of the bizarre affair is, nevertheless, perhaps in order. Early in 1985, in the Paris-based *Messenger of the Russian Christian Movement,* Professor Nikita Struve of the Sorbonne affirmed with great conviction that *Novel with Cocaine,* by one "M. Agheyev," written in the early thirties in Istanbul and published soon thereafter in the Paris émigré review *Numbers,* was in fact the work of Vladimir Nabokov.

To support this thesis, Struve adduced sentences from *Novel with Cocaine* that, according to him, are "typical of Nabokov." Struve's assertions were taken up in a letter to the (London) *Times Literary Supplement,* 9 August 1985, from Julian Graffy of the University of London, who referred to Struve's "detailed analysis of the secondary themes, structural devices, semantic fields [whatever those may be] and metaphors of *N with C,* all of which are found, on the basis of repeated quotation and comparison . . . to be quintessentially Nabokovian."

There have since been other echoes of Struve's theory in several publications in Europe and in the United States.

One can cite numerous deficiencies in Agheyev's style—blatantly incorrect forms, for instance, like *"zachikhnul"* (for "sneezed") or *"ispol 'zovyvat' "* (for "to use")—that are obvious to anyone with a knowledge of Russian. It is amazing that a Sorbonne specialist in Russian language and literature like Struve, or a London University professor of Slavonic studies like Graffy could have confused the incompletely educated Agheyev's often vulgar or incorrect locutions with Nabokov's precise and subtle style. As Dmitri Savitzky notes in an article refuting Struve's theory in *Russian Thought* (Paris, 8 November 1985), Nabokov's Russian possesses the impeccable rhythm of classical poetry, while Agheyev's is "contrived, jolting, uneven." One look at Agheyev's style precludes the need to rebut the rest of Struve's arguments.

In his 1986 book Field ventilates the hypothesis that *Novel with Cocaine* might have been a deliberate mystification by Nabokov or by someone else. He ends by affirming, nonetheless, that "it can be said with absolute certainty . . . that there is *some* link between the work of

Agheyev and Sirin," because there happens to be a par-
tial assonance between the names of Agheyev's character
Sinat[2] and Nabokov's Cincinnatus in *Invitation to a Beheading*.

The Sinat–Cincinnatus connection falls into the same
category of scholarship as, say, Field's overblown claptrap
about an extramarital affair, the total tripe about secret
heavy drinking, the nonsensical conjectures about Father's
death, or the contention that Nabokov, in his letters to
his mother, addressed her as "Lolita" (whereon Field
constructs a typical house of marked cards). In the latter
case his reasoning goes as follows: Father, with the natural
reserve of a gentleman, had preferred to omit the term
of endearment with which he habitually addressed his
mother, whose name was Hélène, from the copies of the
letters he showed to Field before Field revealed his true
colors. Field, after having consumed, I suppose, many
magnifying glasses, gleaned the trace of the "tail or hat"
of a Cyrillic *t* at the edge of the blank space where the
salutation had been excised (incidentally, the handwritten
lowercase Cyrillic *t* generally resembles a small Roman
m, and is, therefore, tailless and hatless). For that reason,
and because the missing word was "about seven letters
long," and also because Father had told him that "Lyolya"

[2]In his story "The Rotten People" originally published (after the novel) under
the offensive title *"Zhid"* ("The Yid"), which, incidentally, Nabokov would
not have used in a million years.

was a perfectly normal Russian diminutive for "Hélène," and God knows for what other reasons, Field concludes (not without a trace of personal outrage), that it was "Lolita, surely," and, characteristically, proceeds to refer to this absurdity as an established fact further on in his book.

Not only does "Lolita" have only six letters; not only would the Latin derivation have been unthinkable within the parameters of Russian etymology, where Spanish cognates did not enjoy the same favor as French or English ones; but the word deleted out of a sense of privacy and out of respect for the memory of a beloved mother was the Russian *"radost' "* ("joy," "dearest"). It was Nabokov's habitual salutation to his mother, and, of course, we have the original letters to prove it. And "Lolita Haze" was "Juanita Dark" in Father's drafts of the novel until very late in the game. So much for "Lolita, surely."

But let us leave Field among his ruins and revisit another corner of the scrap heap briefly to bury the Agheyev matter, whose relevance here is the dramatic dissimilarity between that author's work and *The Enchanter*.

Research by Frank Williams, who originally reviewed the English version of the Agheyev book in the *TLS* on 5 July 1985; by the French literary journalist Alain Garric who went all the way to Istanbul while preparing a lengthy article on the subject for *Libération;* and by others, has confirmed the following sequence of events.

After *Novel with Cocaine* originally appeared in *Numbers* and aroused a certain curiosity in émigré circles, a Russian lady in Paris named Lydia Chervinskaya was asked to track down "Agheyev" with the help of her parents, who happened to live in Istanbul, whence the manuscript had originally been sent. Chervinskaya found him there, confined to a mental institution because of tremors and convulsions. After being rescued by the lady's father, Agheyev became a friend of the family and grew close to Chervinskaya, to whom he confided his real name—Mark Levi—and his complex and motley history, which included the killing of a Russian officer, flight to Turkey, and obsession with drugs.

Levi-Agheyev went with Chervinskaya to Paris but, after a sojourn there, returned to Istanbul, where he died, presumably from the consequences of cocaine abuse, in 1936.

V. S. Yanovsky, who was associated with *Numbers* when the manuscript was first received in Paris, and who now lives in a suburb of New York City, confirmed in an interview reported in *The New York Times* (8 October 1985) that, when the manuscript arrived for publication in Russian, it bore the unequivocally Jewish signature "Levi," and that, somewhere along the line, it was decided to substitute "a more Russian-sounding name." Finally, inquiries by the translator of the French version of the novel that appeared in 1982, cited by Williams, reveal that "a Mark Abramovich Levi was buried in the Jewish cemetery of Istanbul in February 1936."

While no literary adventurer would have a leg to stand on if he were to question the authorship of *The Enchanter,* Professor Struve appears determined to persist in his benighted and quixotic campaign to ascribe the Agheyev work, as well, to VN, who, except for a brief contribution on a very different subject to its first issue, submitted no material to *Numbers,* which had rudely attacked him shortly thereafter; had never visited Moscow, where the novel is set, with a considerable amount of local detail; never used cocaine or other drugs; and wrote, unlike Agheyev, in pure, correct St. Petersburg Russian. Furthermore, if indeed there had been any connection between Nabokov and *Novel with Cocaine,* someone among his literary acquaintances would have had an inkling of it, and, if not, then his wife, first reader, and typist Véra Nabokov would surely have known.

The stucco parapet of the Florida terrace where I am writing at this moment—the kind with white paint covering a deliberately uneven surface—is full of random patterns. It takes only a pencil stroke here and there to complete an excellent hippopotamus, a stern Flemish profile, a busty showgirl, or any number of friendly or disconcerting little free-form monsters.

This is what Nabokov, who early in life had seriously considered becoming a painter, could do so well with an

ornate lampshade, for example, or some repetitively flow-
ered wallpaper. Comical faces, nonexistent but plausible
butterflies, and grotesque little creatures of his own in-
vention gradually came to inhabit hospitable designs of
the quarters at the Montreux-Palace Hotel, where he lived
and worked, and some of them happily survive to this
day, preserved either on our express instructions or by
the limited capacity for observation of the cleaning teams
that storm, like a defensive football line, through those
rooms every afternoon. A few particularly good ones have,
alas, long since been deterged from the tiles adjacent to
the bathtub that, to Field's apparent consternation, Father
used every day.

Such enhancement and recombination of chance patterns are, in a larger sense, an essential part of Nabokov's
creative synthesis. The fortuitous observation, the reported or imagined psychological anomaly, elaborated by
the artist's imagination, assumed a harmonious growth of
their own as the infant work was gradually weaned from
the image, the news item, or the reverie that had jolted
its cells into the process of multiplication.

Like certain of Nabokov's other works, *The Enchanter*
is the study of madness seen through the madman's mind.
Aberrations in general, both physical and psychological,
were among the diverse sources of raw material that nur-
tured Nabokov's artistic fantasy. The criminal pedophilia
of the protagonist—like that of the later Humbert in a
new work and a different setting; like the murderous

delusion of Hermann in *Despair;* like the sexual anomalies that are but one element of *Pale Fire* and other works; like the madness of the chess master Luzhin[3] and the musician Bachmann[4]; like the deformations of the Potato Elf,[5] and of the Siamese twins in "The Double Monster"[6]— was one among many themes Nabokov selected for the creative process of fictional recombination.

> Perhaps what matters is not the human pain or joy at all but, rather, the play of shadow and light on a live body, the harmony of trifles assembled . . . in a unique and inimitable way

writes Nabokov in the concluding sentence of his 1925 short story "The Fight."[7] This early expression, forthright yet undogmatic, of what was to remain an enduring aspect of his aesthetic approach, is, I suspect, destined to be quoted often, and not always in context.

"Perhaps," the word with which Nabokov introduced the thought, is an important qualifier. As a creative writer rather than a journalist, social commentator, or psychoanalyst, Nabokov chose to examine the phenomena of his

[3]In *The Defense,* tr. Michael Scammell, New York, G. P. Putnam's Sons, 1964.
[4]In the short story "Bachmann," in *Tyrants Destroyed and Other Stories,* tr. Dmitri and Vladimir Nabokov, New York, McGraw-Hill, 1975.
[5]In *A Russian Beauty and Other Stories,* tr. Dmitri Nabokov and Simon Karlinsky, New York, McGraw-Hill, 1973.
[6]In "Scenes From the Life of a Double Monster," in *Nabokov's Dozen,* Garden City, New York, Doubleday, 1958.
[7]In *The New Yorker,* tr. Dmitri Nabokov, 18 February 1985.

surroundings through the refractive lens of artistry; at the same time his codex for literary creation is no less precise than the scientific purity of his lepidopterological investigations. But even if his emphasis is on the "combinational delights" in which an artist is privileged to indulge, by no means does it follow that Nabokov was indifferent to the horrors of tyranny, murder, and child molestation; to the tragedy of social or personal injustice; or to the plight of those who have somehow been shortchanged by Fate.

It is not indispensable to have known Father personally in order to understand this; it is enough to have read his books with reasonable care. For the poet in Nabokov the vehicle of choice was the concrete artistic experience rather than the abstract declaration. However, if one is in quest of quotable bits of credo, the miniature Socratic dialogue of the 1927 story "The Passenger"[8] concedes another rare peek into the essence of his ethos. "Life is more talented than we," says the first character, the writer. "How can we compete with that goddess? Her works are untranslatable, indescribable." Hence,

> All that's left to us is to treat her creations as a film producer does a famous novel, altering it beyond recognition . . . for the sole purpose of having an entertaining film unfold without a hitch, punishing virtue in the beginning and vice at the end, . . . with an un-

[8]In *Details of a Sunset and Other Stories,* tr. Dmitri and Vladimir Nabokov, New York, McGraw-Hill, 1976.

expected but all-resolving outcome. . . . We think that
Life's performance is too sweeping, too uneven, that
her genius is too untidy. To indulge our readers we
cut out of Life's untrammeled novels our neat little
tales for the use of schoolchildren. Allow me, in this
connection, to impart to you the following experience. . . .

At the story's end, his interlocutor the wise critic replies:

There is much in life that is casual, and there is also
much that is unusual. The Word is given the sublime
right to enhance chance and to make of the transcen-
dental something that is not accidental.

But the writer's concluding thought expresses two further
distinct, if undivorceable, considerations—artistic curiosity and human compassion:

The trouble is that I did not learn, and shall never
learn, why the passenger cried.

One suspects, early on in *The Enchanter,* that things
will not end well, that the cynical, contemptible protagonist will get his due, and, if an obvious moral is needed,
this premonition is it. However, besides being part horror
story, this is also part mystery thriller: Fate toys with the
madman, now thwarting, now abetting, now providing
a hair-raising close call; as events unfold we do not yet
know from which direction disaster will strike, but we
sense increasingly that it is imminent.

The man is a dreamer like others, although in this case a very rotten dreamer. Distasteful as he may be, though, one of the most poignant levels of this story is that of his—occasionally objective—introspection. One might even go so far as to say that the story resides in the introspection; and through this introspection on the basically evil protagonist's part Nabokov succeeds in transmitting compassion not only for the victims but, to a degree, for the villain himself. A yearning for decency gleams now and then through the man's single-minded cynicism, and prompts pathetic attempts at self-justification; although the borderlines dissolve under the impetus of his compulsion, he cannot escape the fleeting realization that he is a monster. And while the woman he marries may be a repellent means to a criminal end, and the girl an instrument for his gratification, other nuances emerge. The viewpoint of the text—like many other aspects of the story—may sometimes be deliberately ambiguous, but the madman himself cannot avoid perceiving, in stunned moments of lucidity, the pathetic side of both mother and daughter. His pity for the former transpires, with a kind of reverse Russian, through the very revulsion on which he harps; and there is a moving instant of compassion when we see her, through his eyes, as pregnant "with her own death." As for the girl, there exists a fragile, decent sliver of his soul that *would like to feel* a genuinely paternal love for her.

The Enchanter, evil conjuror though he may be, lives partially in an enchanted world. And, common madman or not, he perceives himself on a special, poetic plane as a mad king (for he knows that he is, in any case, mad)— a king who is fleetingly reminiscent of other, thematically related, lone Nabokovian monarchs and is, at the same time, a kind of lecherous Lear living in fairy-tale seclusion by the sea with his "little Cordelia," whom, for a flicker of an instant, he imagines as an innocent, innocently loved daughter. But, as always, the paternal shades rapidly into the infernal, and the beast within him plunges into a pedophilic fantasy so intense that its consequences cause a female fellow-passenger to change compartments.

In agonizing moments of introspection he recognizes the beast and tries to will it away. Ingeniously appropriate images recur in bestial counterpoint—hyenas in every hygiene; onanistic tentacles; the lupine leer in place of the intended smile; the licking of chops at the thought of his defenseless, sleeping prey; the whole leitmotif of the Wolf about to devour his Red Riding Hood, complete with its eerie final echo. This dark beast within him, this bête noire of his, must always be construed as the protagonist's implicit self-perception, and, in his rational moments, it is what the Enchanter fears most; thus, catching himself in an absentminded smile, he posits, with pathetic, flimsy hope, that "only *humans* are capable of absentmindedness" and that therefore he too might after all be human.

The stratification of the story is most striking in its double- and triple-bottomed imagery. It is true, in a sense, that some delicate passages are more explicit than elsewhere in Nabokov. But at other moments the sexual undercurrent is no more than the glinting facet of a simile or the momentary derailment of a train of thought headed for a quite different destination. Multiple levels and senses, as is known, occur often in Nabokov. Yet the line he treads here is razor thin, and the virtuosity consists in a deliberate vagueness of verbal and visual elements whose sum is a complex, otherwise undefinable, but totally precise unit of communication.

An analogous kind of ambiguity, whose purpose and synthesis are again the exact expression of a complex concept, is at times employed to convey the concurrent— and conflicting—thoughts racing through the protagonist's brain. As a limpid instance of what I mean, let me cite one such passage, whose paradoxes, at first sight, challenge reader and translator alike, but, when approached without selectively closing the switch on tracks of thought parallel to what at first seems the main line, again reward one with a crystalline whole that is greater than the sum of its parts; the openness of receptivity required here, which would perhaps represent overkill in dealing with more conventional writing, is akin to that which a sensitive ear will apply to the counterpoint of Bach or the thematic texture of Wagner, or which a stubborn eye will force upon a recalcitrant brain when their possessor perceives that the same elements of a tricky design can simultaneously yield, say, an ape peering wistfully out of its cage and a beach ball bobbing, hopelessly out of reach, amid the reflections of a sunset on the repetitious ripples of an azure sea.

The protagonist, rather than face his odious nuptial obligations, has gone roaming in the night. He has considered various alternatives of disposing of his newly acquired, already superfluous spouse, who is promisingly ill, but every moment of whose existence keeps him from the girl he craves. He has pondered poison, presumably entered a pharmacy, perhaps made a purchase. On his return he sees a strip of light under the door of the "dear departed" and says to himself, "Charlatans . . . We'll have to stick to the original version." The concurrent ideas here can be listed thus:

1. He is disappointed that she has not gone to sleep.
2. He had half-consciously been equating sleep with death.
3. Our seeing her, through his eyes, as the "dear departed" connotes his sarcastic reaction to her being
    a. awake
    b. alive.
4. Or the term "dear departed" signifies that, in his mind, she is already dead or as good as dead.

5. He must now either satisfy his unappetizing bride or find a plausible excuse to say good night and go to bed (the "original version").
6. His access to the girl remains as problematic as ever.
7. The "charlatans" are
   a. the pharmacists whose potion he did not buy;
   b. the pharmacists whose potion he did buy but did not use;
   c. the pharmacists whose potion his obsessed imagination has meanwhile administered, expecting to find the woman dead, equating, as we have seen, wakefulness with life (for "pharmacists" read the whole establishment of forensic medicine that has somehow let him down);
   d. the pangs of conscience and/or fear that have made him discard the idea of poison and/or murder in general; or
   e. the hope against hope that he has succeeded in simply willing her demise.
8. All of the above merge in the kaleidoscope of a mad mind.

Did the man actually enter the pharmacy? Here, as elsewhere, my translatorial ethics would prohibit adding to Father's text to make things more explicit in English than they are in Russian. The text's multilevel, pleasingly elliptical form is an integral part of its character. If VN had wanted to be more specific here, he would have done so in the original.

Time and place are purposely left imprecise in the story, which is essentially timeless and placeless. One might presume that the 1930s are nearly over, and, as Nabokov later confirmed,[9] that we are in Paris, and then en route to the south of France. There is also a brief detour to a small city not very far from the capital. The only character mentioned by name in the text[10] is the least important one: the female servant, in that provincial city, who helps the ill-fated child pack and shoos away the chicks as the car, containing protagonist and prey united at last, speeds away.

I shall leave to the studious—among whom exist some superbly sensitive readers of Nabokov—the detailed identification and the documentation of themes and levels (straight narrative, tricky metaphor, romantic poetry, sexuality, fairy-tale sublimation, mathematics, conscience, compassion, fear of being strung up by the heels), as well as the search for hidden parallels with *The Song of Igor's Campaign* or *Moby Dick*. Father would have put Freudians

[9] See Author's Note One.
[10] For a name Nabokov subsequently attributed to the protagonist, see Author's Note One and p. 101, ll. 18–24.

on guard against rejoicing at the ephemeral mention of a sister, the girl's curious regression into infancy at the end, or the elaborate walking stick (which *is* unabashedly and entertainingly phallic but, on a totally distinct plane, visually evocative as well of the appetizing, "valuable" objects—another example is the rare, blank-faced watch— with which Nabokov sometimes liked to endow his characters).

Certain other compressed images and locutions should, possibly, be explained, since it would be a pity if they were wasted. Here are a few "special" examples, given, unlike those singled out above, in proper order.

The "black salad devouring a green rabbit" (p. 25, l. 11): one of a number (see below) of visual aberrations that, on one level, give the story a surreal, enchanted aura while, on another, describing with utmost economy and directness how a character's perception of reality is momentarily distorted by a state of being (in this case, the protagonist's overpowering, thwarted, barely concealed excitement).

The "little Japanese steps" (p. 27, l. 2): many if not all readers must have seen, on the big screen or the little one, or at the opera, or perhaps in the real Orient, the geisha-style walk—short, mincing steps on high platform sandals—to which Nabokov likens the girl's progress on skates whose wheels refuse to roll on the gravel.

A potentially more cryptic passage is that of the "strange,

nailless finger" scrawled on the fence (p. 42, l. 15). Here, again, deliberate ambiguity, concurrent images and ideas, and multiple levels of interpretation are at play. To spell this one out: The "definite goal" that emerges from a substratum of the man's brain is access to the girl via marriage to the mother. The imagined graffito on the fence is a hybrid of the forefinger pointing the way on old-fashioned signs and of some joker's phallic doodle that the digit's stylized, nailless shape simultaneously suggests to a mind bent, basically, on depravity, but not devoid of self-reproaching flashes of objectivity. This ambiguous finger simultaneously indicates, in the fleeting image, the path of courtship (of the mother), the secret parts of the yearned-for girl, and the protagonist's own vulgarity that no amount of rationalization can explain away.

"Cuff" (p. 44, l. 21) as in "cuff links." It is clearly implied that the poor woman is still playing hard to get. The wordplay, with an oblique echo of the work's Russian title, whose most direct meaning is "magician," refers to a card up the conjuror's sleeve—the superficial trappings of marriage—plus the actual, live, presumably loving husband, "the live ace of hearts." There is also a parallel, introspective nuance here: the cynical trick that this travesty of a marriage represents to the protagonist. He shares this underlying joke with the perceptive reader, though not, of course, with his bride-to-be. We have the same kind of multiple compression here as in the graffito image.

"Compass rose" (p. 50, l. 7): The early Italian nautical compass card, more stylized than today's, and indicating, as compass roses still do, the principal and subsidiary compass points (which also identified the directions from which winds blew) was called *rosa dei venti*, "rose of the winds," because of its flowerlike appearance and because wind directions were of paramount concern to navigators; the Italian term survives to this day. A nice fillip is gained in translation (for a minority of readers perhaps—those who navigate and those who know Italian), since the image refers to drafts coming from various directions through windows opened by the charwoman.

"The 32nd" (p. 50, l. 8): another beautifully concentrated image that it is almost a pity to deaden by bookish explication. His violent emotions—anticipation of finally encountering the girl alone, the infuriating surprise and disappointment of finding the bustling char—have simply imparted a moist blur to his vision and made him see an absurd date. The month is immaterial. A Nabokovian irony is there, but a bit of compassion for the monster seeps through as well.

A "doubling cat" (p. 81, l. 11) is a cat seen by a child so tired that she has difficulty keeping her eyes focused. It is, optically, akin to "the 32nd" and the "green rabbit."

It would of course have been possible to give a minute explanation of every challenging passage, but that would have produced a scholarly apparatus longer than the text itself. These little puzzles, which, without exception, have an artistic purpose, should also be fun. The approximate reader, drowsy from the airliner's unhealthy air and the complimentary drinks he has downed, always has the lamentable option of skipping, as he often did with the best-selling *Lolita.*

The things *I* love about the story are, among others, the suspense (how will reality betray the dream?) and the corollary of a surprise on every page; the eerie humor (the grotesque wedding night; the suspicious chauffeur who vaguely foreshadows Clare Quilty; the Shakespearean clown of a night porter; the protagonist's desperate search for the misplaced room—will he emerge, as in "A Visit to the Museum,"[11] into a totally different town or will the old porter, whom he comes upon at last, react as if seeing him for the first time in his life?); the descriptions (the forest hopping from hill to hill only to trip over the highway, and much else); the preliminary glimpses of people and things with a parallel life of their own that will, incidentally or crucially, recur; the trucks ominously thundering in the night; the splendidly innovative use of Russian in the original; the cinematic imagery of the surreal conclusion and the frenzied pace, a kind of *stretta finale,* that accelerates toward the crashing climax.

The English title chosen by Father has, of course, a

[11]In *A Russian Beauty and Other Stories,* tr. Dmitri Nabokov and Simon Karlinsky, New York, McGraw-Hill, 1973.

not-so-secret echo in The Enchanted Hunters of *Lolita*. I shall leave to others the search for additional Easter eggs of this kind as well. One should be wary, however, of exaggerating the significance of superficial similarities. Nabokov considered *The Enchanter* a totally distinct work, only distantly connected to *Lolita*. It may have contained, as he put it, "the first little throb" of the later novel— and even that thesis might be questioned if one attentively examines certain earlier works of his—but we must also not forget that the arts in general pulsate with first throbs that foreshadow future, larger works; various literary compositions come to mind, such as Joyce's *Portrait of the Artist*. Or, conversely, there may be a subsequent mini-version, a final distillation such as Massenet's *Portrait of Manon*. In any case, *Volshebnik* is certainly not a *Portrait of Lolita:* the differences between the two are clearly greater than the similarities. Whether or not the later novel is a love affair between the author and the English language, a love affair between Europe and America, a jaundiced view of the motel scene and the surrounding landscape, a modern-day "free translation of *Onegin*" (these and a multitude of other hypotheses have been advanced, eagerly but with varying degrees of seriousness and credibility), *Lolita* is unquestionably the product of very new and different artistic stimuli.

On the premise that it is preferable to be angelic than foolish in approaching the genesis of a complex artistic work, I shall not venture to assess the importance to *Lolita* of Nabokov's study of Lewis Carroll; of his observations in Palo Alto in 1941; or of Havelock Ellis's transcription, circa 1912, of a Ukrainian pedophile's confessions, which have been translated from the original French by Donald Rayfield (who, despite a haunting echo of the fictional John Ray, Jr., Ph.D., in *Lolita,* is a very real British scholar). Rayfield theorizes, amid certain less convincing assertions, that the pseudonymous Victor, via Ellis, deserves credit "for his contribution to the theme and plot of *Lolita* and the strange sensuous and intellectual character of Humbert Humbert, the hero of Nabokov's finest English-language novel." And, while acknowledging the previous composition of *The Enchanter* (whose title he translates literally as "The Magician"), he further conjectures that the unfortunate Ukrainian's account provided the final impetus for the emergence of "*Lolita*'s central theme."[12] This hypothesis might merit consideration, were it not for certain chronological facts that I must nevertheless point out: It was not until 1948 that Edmund Wilson sent the Ellis transcription to Nabokov, who had had no previous acquaintance with it—while *Volshebnik,* which does contain what might be called the "central theme" (if little else) of *Lolita,* was completed in 1939.

[12]I am indebted, for certain details and citations, to Edwin McDowell's report in *The New York Times* of 15 March 1985, regarding the publication by Grove Press of *The Confessions of Victor X.*

As for *The Enchanter*'s contribution, occasional ideas and images from it are indeed echoed in *Lolita*. But, as I—and many others—have noted in the past, themes and details of various kinds often recur in Nabokov's novels, stories, poems, and plays. In this case, the echoes are distant and the dissimilarities substantial: setting (geographically but, above all, artistically remote); characters (reflected on occasion, but dimly at best); development and dénouement (totally different).

Perhaps a girl in a European park, fleetingly recalled by Humbert on an early page of *Lolita*, is Nabokov's way of acknowledging the little heroine of *The Enchanter,* but also of relegating her forever to the category of very distant relative.

Dolores Haze may, as Nabokov says, be "very much the same lass" as the Enchanter's victim, but only in an inspirational, conceptual sense. In other ways the earlier child is very different—perverse only in the madman's eyes; innocently incapable of anything like the Quilty intrigue; sexually unawakened and physically immature, which is perhaps why Weidle recalled her as a ten-year-old.

It would be a serious mistake to roll away, on that protonymphet's skates, into a garden of parallel primrose paths.